The Magritte Poems

Mark Young

Sandy Press

Contents

cont'd

cont'd

cont'd

cont'd

cont'd

                                                          cont'd

cont'd

                                                cont'd

cont'd

Roman numbers following a poem's title mean that this is one of a number of paintings by Magritte that have the same title. The inclusion of a year after the title usually means the same thing; but occasionally is used to simply indicate that this is an early painting. A Hindu / Arabic number after the title means that there are other poems here with the same title. The use of English or French titles — & a Dutch one — simply depends what language was used when I first came across the painting.

M. Y.

INTRODUCTION

tin painted impossible greens we all knew meant grass —
meant, was not. Illusion wasn't part of the game.
— Gerald Burns

The poems presented here by Mark Young are a response to the paintings of his beloved Belgian painter, the Surrealist René Magritte (1898–1967). Young, born in New Zealand, and having made Australia his home since 1969, long-time, and erudite editor of *Otoliths*, is a prolific poet of great standing, with more than seventy publications to his name. The language of the poet in this collection hosts free verse everywhere, from puzzles-as-poems, such as "Memory (1948)," which resembles Lewis Carroll's nineteenth-century doublets, as described in *Vanity Fair*, to chessboards ("The Loftiest Game"), to collaged form guides ("COUNTRY RACING / ROCKHAMPTON," "Magritte"), to the chant of Surrealist techniques, such as automatic writing, and collage, to prose poetry, to poems that look like market surveys or online auctions, and blogging ("Confiture de Cheval" — horses are recurring motifs, "The Torturing of the Vestal Virgin," *etc.*), to numerous experiments with typography ("An Advertisement for Norine (Lord Lister variant)," "Querelle des universaux," "The Night Owl," *etc.*). This makes reading Young's poetry very engaging. But poet and painter, are they the same thing? Are their aims the same? Young shows in his poetry that he is not merely being descriptive of Magritte's work, though he sprinkles the common images of the bowler hat, the apple (trees), leaves (trees again), clouds, birds (in trees), horses and their bells, the smoker's pipe, mirrors, windows, the sea and sky, *etc.* Magritte's hats were contemporaneous, painted in an era they were worn, not like today when you hardly see a hat (maybe a baseball cap, worn as intended, or inverted — here Young is able to get mention of Donald Trump in). Some words or images are immediately associated with their artist, such as "calligramme" with Apollinaire, "*duende*" with Lorca, the bowler hat with Magritte, "readymade" with Duchamp, *etc.* They're like signatures or shorthand. Magritte, and consequently, Young, employ the *bilboquet* often as a symbol. The dictionary definition of *bilboquet* is a cup-and-ball game, but it has also been identified as a bowling pin or even baluster in the case of Magritte, whereas Young makes use of the ambiguity here by suggesting it is a type of bird early on in his poetry, before going on to describe it as chess pieces, "phallustrades" ("The Married Priest"), and something that floats, like a duck, I suppose. However, the important thing to note is, it's all a *game*. ("Décalcomanie," the title of a poem in this collection, is also a game favored by the Surrealists, one that relies on chance, and is, ironically, stochastic; ironic, for etymologically, "stochastic" is "skillful with one's aim.") Flemish painters painted the same thing as Magritte did (Magritte was primarily a painter, however, he also wrote), but just as Magritte saw what they saw but through a new lens, so too does Young in his poetry. "The Married Priest" illustrates all of Magritte's obsessions (a deliberately repetitive vocabulary, a rhetorical device):

> Over & over. Re-
> peating the images.
> Replaying them, the
> same, a different
> game. Con text

Young ends on "the apples / might wear a mask" in this poem. The repeated images may be in "homage" to Magritte's "limited palette," *i.e.*, constraints, although Young uses all the modernist, and postmodernist devices available to him. Barthes claims that the "obsessive would experience the voluptuous release of the letter," the epistemology of "the words / that hide behind the words be- / hind the mask" ("Le Masque Vide"). Young's sense of mystery is like Magritte's, at once familiar yet strange:

> The sorcery
> lies in an operation rendered
>   invisible by the simplicity
>   of its result — "The Two Mysteries (2)," using the

postmodernist technique of sourcing the text from *This Is Not a Pipe* by Michel Foucault (Young dedicates "The Betrayal of Images (2)" to Foucault), and *The Ladies' Book of Etiquette* by Florence Hartley (published in 1860).

Young also likes to make the familiar unfamiliar, as when he mixes up aphorisms or common sayings ("which came first, the / candle or the eggs," "La Veillée," or "Beauty is in the eye of the bullholder," "Pour devenir un fort soldat / To become a strong soldier (1918)" — "prosodic rhythms, of [quoted] truisms" — Barthes). Just as Magritte plays with semiotics, so does Young — Magritte's most famous work is *The Betrayal of Images*, perhaps because of the words *"Ceci n'est pas une pipe"* (I even saw "CECI N'EST PAS UN PALAIS" graffitied on a factory wall in Potsdam), repeated in an English version. The differentiation between the object (signifier) and the representation of that object (signified):

> Sweet Jesus. *Le fils de l'homme*
> as a skateboard. What would
> Foucault have made of this,
> especially since the constructors
> insist *ceci n'est pas un skateboard?* — "Skate / parked /
> bored,"

and

> Ceci n'est pas
> une pipe. N'est
> pas ceci aussi. Only
> the painting is /
> what it claims
> to be. Is a
> painting. Is
> a painting of
> a pipe. Or in
> this case also
> a painting of
> a painting of
> a pipe. — "The Two Mysteries (1)"

Young sometimes circumscribes Magritte; *The Son of Man* is a Magritte title that Young has used in his poem. Magritte says, "Here we have the apparent visible, the apple, hiding the hidden visible, the person's face" — in case we don't see the Apollinarian connection with the symbol of the apple, he spells it out in words; as Young says in "The Music Lesson," "in / part a kind of signifier." Magritte used words and images in his work of the late 1920s — he listed eighteen points of significance about relationships between word and image, the seventh being apposite to Young: "A word can take the place of an object in reality." The apotheosis of this is *The Betrayal of Images*. The reason language works is *agreement* — we agree that this fruit is an apple (in English, *pomme* in French, *yabloko* in Russian, *ringo* in Japanese, *etc.*). Young disrupts this agreement in order to heighten language, make us sit up and take note. The shock of language. In "Elective Affinities," we see Young's and Magritte's "systematic search for 'affinities' between objects":

A civil
celebrant, Magritte,
a union-
maker, who brings
disparate things
together &
creates an arc
that leaps the
gap between
them. On
one hand.
On the other.
Relationships
exist, affinities
not always ob-
vious. & yet so
obvious. Such
as that which he has
elected to display
here. But sparks
still fly. So might
the egg if
re-
leased
from the cage. — "Elective Affinities"

Marriage as an affinity. Interstices. Enjambment. The line or hyphen that leads one astray; a *trait d'union* is the French for hyphen, where "union" is used ambiguously:

The male	There it
flower	encounters
breaks off	the female.
& rises	
to the	Birds
surface of	grow.
the water.	
	The use

of hyphens with adverbs is redundant
unless an identical adjective exists.

Late-blooming sun. — "Le Trait d'union"

Barthes, in *The Pleasure of the Text* (the pleasure of writing, its rules, its grammar — "Some *trompe- / l'oeil*. Much grammar," "The Marches of Summer"), asks if "today's writer [is not] the residual substitute for the beggar, the monk, the bonze: unproductive, but nevertheless provided for[.] Analogous to the Buddhist sangha." Early in Young's career, he worked in the Japanese embassy in Wellington — you can see the Japanese influence in "The literal meaning of *jan / ken pon*, the Japanese equi- / valent of rock, scissors, paper, / is 'beginning with stone'" ("The Gradation of Fire"), the mantra in "Meditation" ("*I go for refuge in the Sangha*"). or the mention of Hokusai (master printmaker), and Yoshitsune (samurai) in "La Cascade." Young is exploring "the *deceptive* nature of literature" (Barthes, with emphasis in the original). As Barthes (again) says, "text itself is atopic."

Popular culture, mass culture, social media, the Internet age, computers, consumerist jargon, production, globalization, news headlines, are Young's material for his poetry, in this book, and in many others. They add to the drama, and they are a new way of seeing. His poetry abounds with references to Amazon, the Apple Store, eBay, Photoshop, KFC, McDonald's, Starbucks, Snapchat, Windows, AI, the

Oscars, Sherlock Holmes, Miley Cyrus, The Poynter Sisters, Harrison Ford, James Dean, Gameboy, YouTube, Helen Mirren, the films *Brazil*, *My Fair Lady*, and *Eyes Wide Shut*, Fellini, Alfred Hitchcock, Twentieth Century Fox, Frank Sinatra, Fred Astaire, Gloria Swanson, Led Zeppelin, the songs "I Am What I Am," "It's Raining Men," "Summertime," "Time after Time," *etc.* (including the snatch *"Voulez-vous coucher avec moi, ce soir?"* from Lady Marmalade), Leonard Cohen, k. d. lang, Michael Jackson, Gérard Depardieu, Radiohead, The Rolling Stones, robots, Prince Charming, *The Art of War*, Irving Berlin, Sean Connery, David Bowie, Marlene Dietrich, Iggy Pop, Ursula Le Guin, Samuel R. Delaney, Lee Harvey Oswald, QR-codes, COVID-19 (just once), the Titanic, Yoko Ono, and Kim Kardashian. Everything is fair game, even Science Fiction. The (pseudo-)science of "La Gravitation Universelle," or quoting Simone Weil ("All the / natural movements of the soul / are controlled by laws analogous / to those of physical gravity," "The State of Grace"), or "a Foucault test us[ing] interference patterns produced by a knife edge / to determine the deviation of a mirror from its ideal shape / Foucault the first to show how a pendulum can track Earth's rotation / mechanisms acting during human sleep" ("An End To Contemplation," where Foucault is not Michel but Léon). Barthes calls it "the knife of value" or "the zero of the signified." The truism of "Returning to the Moon is the key to humanity's long-term future in space" ("Clear Ideas"), yet every syllable in Young's poetry is essential. He uses simple language to discuss complex ideas, even when the vocabulary may be hit or miss (he refers to his lecture "Stochastic Acts" in "La Cascade," his version of *How I Wrote Certain of My Books*, but in such a casual way typical of his writing, where readers may or may not pick up on his associations: "A massive earthquake. A tropical cyclone. A picture of Hokusai. Stochastic acts"). The typical Young device of mixing science with popular culture: "Lotka & Volterra, with the ratio of yin to yang determining who is / x & y in the differentiated equation" ("The Spy"), or "This is a piece of the old Atomium, in the Delft University of / Technology" ("This is a Piece of Cheese," dedicated to Yoko Ono). Young also luxuriates in the pleasure of paronomasia: "I took my troubles / down to Mme / Gorgon. Zola" ("Le Philtre"), "Ceci est un morceau de fromage," "La Marchande de Sable" (Le Marchand de Sel or The Saltseller was an anagrammatic nickname Marcel Duchamp had for himself), "condom/inium" ("La Belle idée"), "archi- / texture" ("The Song of Love"), "Bored games" ("Checkmate"), "In this fromage to / Jacques Louis David" ("Madame Récamier de David (1)"), "the bland leading the / bland" ("Le Masque Vide"), *etc.*

Lewis Carroll was in the mind of Magritte as well as Young, who often undercuts his subjects with the absurd: "Alice, Albert / Einstein, & Annie / Edson Taylor, the first / person to go over / Niagara Falls in a / barrel" ("Perpetual Motion (1)"), or

> Given a list
> of words. Asked
> to repeat them
> back. A test
> for veridical
> memory. Eye,
> reflection, looking-
> & cheval-glass,
> sky. Alice. All
> synonyms of. Or.
> Associated with.
> Not included. Her
> initial answer. The
> thought made
> visible. Mirror. — "The False Mirror (2)"

Alice's Adventures in Wonderland was beloved by the Surrealists. Young's disruption of syntax is a similar declaration of a way of seeing. While other poets explore the humor in the juxtaposition of high and low culture, Young always remains ironical.

While the vocation, the art of the artist is in the present, even when painted or composed long ago, the reader or viewer is always in the future. Sometimes the art itself is in a further future, even if the reader or viewer cannot accept it as such. (A future that is always unfinished, like life itself: "[Composition on a Sea Shore]" is the only poem that is deliberately left unfinished at the end, in future time, like life itself.) However, Young addresses the future in several of his poems: "The Window (2)," "L'Avenir" (The Future), "Clear Ideas," "The Listening Room (1958)," "The Future of Statues," "The Threatened Assassin,"

"Fortune Telling," "The Denizens of the River," *etc.* There were those when photography was a new art who said about painting, "Why bother? Photography can reproduce the landscape just as well, if not better." (The same can be said today of artificial intelligence.) Both may coexist — it's the imagination that is paramount, and critical; the rest is just mechanics.

For more than a century, the dream has been considered legitimate pabulum for the artist. While many people see landscape or the city as the place of creativity or the imagination, rather than seeing a single artist, others see that image, and imagery belong to artists, poet and painter alike (what Baudelaire called the "cult of images"). But it is true that the Muse, Mnemosyne, belongs in the past rather than the future. Ambrose Bierce, in his *Devil's Dictionary*, defined imagination as "A warehouse of facts, with poet and liar in joint ownership." A warehouse of images, moreover.

We lose ourselves in the imagination, inspiration, and *daimon* of the artist — imaginary scenes or historical scenes, scenes how the artist imagined they appeared, abstractions, repetition. We investigate the interior of ourselves. We go for a walk, which inspires us to paint, to write, to make permanent that which is not. Magritte, like many artists, including Niek Kemps's ambiguity/obscurity, was trying to say when he painted a version of *The Birth of Venus* that, like Benjamin, and Goethe before him, beauty is not a covering, the shell, not even Venus personified, but an essence. A transformation takes place. That is what Young is trying to capture.

The circularity of nature: landscape, panorama, trees, forest, sky, the sea, *etc.* Nature has to be transformed, either physically, when we make cities, human constructions, *etc.*, and in art, where it is a type of mimesis. Barthes said, reality is "suspended between," where Bachelard saw the philosophy of imagination as an adjective, *i.e.*, as part of grammar, as part of language. Charles Bernstein, speaking as a poet, and conscious of what Adorno had to say about history, said it was important not to aestheticize, symptomatize, territorialize or ideologize imagination but, as part of imagination's circumference, its creativity, to essentialize it. Young uses language, spectacle, imagination, knowledge, insight, invention, memory, curiosity, character, and poetry in order to transfigure the baseness of life, its vulgarities, its violence, its ugliness;

26

he transcends them with language. The difference between imaginary and imagination. The transitivity, and performativity of imagination. While the painter may produce optical illusions (in person, Magritte's attire is iconic, sculptural; in painting, it is symbolic, semiotic), the poet produces poetical allusions. Just as Magritte used objects out of context in his paintings, Young does so with words. In "Le Prisonnier," he explains: "It's probably something I / learnt from — copied from? — / Magritte, the giving of titles that bear no relation to the item in question." Paradoxically, putting inspiration into practice is the ordering of chaos. Inspiration is light, the sun, reflection. It is a game. It is an artifice. Young addresses environmental issues in his latter poems. He adopts Coleridge's "secondary imagination," *i.e.*, dissolves, diffuses, dissipates, in order to re-create."

Young explains in "The Month of the Grape Harvest (2)" that

> Anything can be
> connected to anything else —
> that's an underlying principle
> of hermetic semiosis

This is not merely a homage to a painter. Young articulates Magritte's experience in "The Great War I"; he is indirect in his pacifism, but direct in his condemnation of colonialism. He mixes Magritte's biography (his wife, Georgette, the suicide of his mother, *etc.*) with his own autobiography (mention of "Magritte in North Queensland", his age, his father, "Stochastic Acts", and a fondness for detective fiction, which he shared with Magritte, with dedications to Dashiell Hammett and Jo Nesbø; Fantômas, that charming criminal eluding justice). "Cicerone," his longest poem in the collection, is hardly autobiographical, however, for it is Incan in nature; Machu Picchu, its citadel, the site of the priest as well as the poet. In "Clear Ideas," Young says "The sea is its avatar" — "its" could be human endeavor, such as going to the moon. He concludes by asking in "Checkmate," "Am I his avatar?" You be the judge.

— Javant Biarujia
South Yarra, July 26, 2024

The Son of Man (3)

I put on
a bowler hat

take an apple
for lunch

& head for
la plage at

Yeppoon
where I en-

gage in
a bit of

plagiarism by
purloining the i-

mages of Magritte
& putting

them forward
as my own.

Not to be Reproduced

Shown from the back
the image is androgynous - think
k.d.lang in her man's suit
phase. It is a portrait of the artist
as a young (wo)man. It is not
a portrait of the artist. Magritte says
it is not to be reproduced
though he reproduces it
anyway. We do not see
the face. Magritte does not
produce it. Or reproduce it.
Is not reflected in the mirror
for what comes back from there
is not mirror-image
but reproduction. Almost as if
we were peering over a shoulder
only to see the shoulder that we
were peering over. But it is
reflection. The mantlepiece
is reflected & the copy of
Edgar Allan Poe's *Adventures
of Arthur Gordon Pym* that rests
upon it is partially reflected. It
is a book about an imaginary
journey. Magritte's painting
is a journey of imagination
about what happens between
two points that are the same point
though there is distance
between them. He says it is not to be
reproduced. It is reproduced here.

Le Somnambule

It should have been a one-
pipe problem, Watson, but
my sleep patterns have been
irregular lately, have moved
from the no sleep of cocaine
use to an ersatz sleepwalking,
full of fear, as if the hound of
the Baskervilles was hard on

my heels. I wake, immediately
reach for another pipe. Have
lost count of how many I've
smoked in the last few weeks.
& now I'm having visions,
will suddenly see an owl in my
chair, my pipe in its mouth; &
we have moved from Baker

Street to somewhere in the
country. & the owl peers at me
through its saucer eyes, takes
the pipe out of its mouth, looks
down at it & says to me: "This is
not a pipe." & what it means by
that, Watson, is the problem. Is
beyond my sphere of expertise.

Les Pierreries

So much alike as
we peer from the
box we could
pass as brothers.

But what's in a
box is often more
than just contain-
ment, what reso-

nates can be more
than *beauty is*. Gems
we might some-
times be referred

to as; but what
other facets will
be displayed when
the lid is lifted?

La Joconde (1962)

The slice-of-sky curtain is
center stage — or should
that be center *plage*? Behind

it are two other curtains, red
this time, ready, when the
bell starts to ring, to move

slightly forward & draw to-
gether to conceal the other &
leave only sand & sea in sight.

Do not remove all the chairs

The pipe is overhead. Free from all disc-
ursive attachment, it can float anew in
its natural silence. Make no mistake,
nothing is easier to recognize than a pipe.
This is the first rule to be observed. The

second? Never sit down to the piano unin-
vited, unless you are alone in the parlor. An
old custom not without basis, because the
entire function is so scholarly as to allow
the object it represents to appear without

hesitation or equivocation. & the third? The
small articles of a wardrobe require constant
care. Should be of such material as will bear
the crush of a crowded store without injury.
A dignified, modest reserve is the surest way

to repel impertinence. No truer remark was
ever made. In vain the text unfurls below
the drawing with all the attentive fidelity
of a label in a scholarly book. A figure in
the shape of writing. The image of a text.

Sources:
This Is Not a Pipe, by Michel Foucault
The Ladies' Book of Etiquette (1860), by Florence Hartley

Collage (Sur L'Oiseau Mort) (1926)

The silhouette of a man's
head has the cutout of
a bilboquet within it.

Pinions a dead bird, an
image also found in a
painting done the same

year. A whiff of sadism
to them — the sparrow
usually emblematic of

fragility but here associ-
ated with a violent death.
Who knows what angst

remained in the painter's
heart: but ever since, most of
his birds were live & white.

Portrait de Commandant Marius Delsaux (1923)

No need to flee to Canada
to avoid *les rigueurs* of
military service
                when you
have artistic ability of such
an high level that a portrait

                                of your commanding officer
                            promotes you to an alternative
                                method of serving the
                                        military —
                        painting portaits of the remain-
                        der of the garrison officer corps.

Observation #5

I have just posted *L'Ovation*, poem number 500 in my *Series Magritte*, & am taking this milestone as a place to pause & review my endeavors. What concerns me is that the trope may be somewhat passé — after all, I haven't seen anyone wearing a bowler hat for at least 60 years.

Fill / loosely & / do not compact

With experience, this copper-alloy piece can be used to create a product that includes all the processes involved in harvesting, production, transportation, & construction. It eliminates all extremes of elaboration, but forces you to leave behind your familiar house, street, & neighbors; & prompts a defection from fixed meaning through the use of non-sequiturs — start off with Magritte & move on to the navigational abilities of the prostate, from Derrida on to the venture capital industry.

Be careful, when traveling, not to wound the feelings of your friends

I cannot dismiss the notion that
the sorcery here lies in an opera-
tion rendered invisible by the
simplicity of its result. We must
assume, I believe, that a calligram

has formed, then unraveled. I can-
not too severely censure the habit
of using sentences which admit of
a double meaning. The calligram
is thus tautological. Cleverly ar-

ranged on a sheet of paper, signs
invoke the very thing of which
they speak. Every conversation is
considered in a measure confident-
ial. To be able to converse really

well, you must read much, treasure
in your memory the pearls of what
you read, profit from the extra rich-
ness of language that allows us to say
different things with a single word.

Sources:
This Is Not a Pipe, by Michel Foucault
The Ladies' Book of Etiquette (1860), by Florence Hartley

Après le bal

In more modern times it would
be *My Fair Lady*. "I could have
danced all night, & still come back
for more." Or maybe not. Naked
on a bed, asleep. Not so much a
bed but a plinth. & she obviously
worn out, comfort not a consider-
ation. & the curtain that partitions
now from before drawn back to
reveal a destruction that has not
necessarily paused, houses on their
sides, the floor of the room, the out-
side, those hills beyond, all cracked
beyond repair, bilboquets run amok,
fallen into the grass or still flying
around. But this is back then, back
when the phonograph was barely
invented, & she no untouched Aphro-
dite but fully formed, fully conscious —
though unconscious — of her surrounds.
No seashore, no halfshell, no cherubs,
just somewhere offstage a disenchanted
Pygmalion translating some sheet
music to an upright piano & singing
to himself the before of it. "Down fell
the glass dear, broken, that's all,
just as my heart was after the ball."

Tête d'homme (1920)

There is always a
before, he said, but
let your imagination

shape what comes
after, even if you had-
n't planned a head.

The Improvement

Things might seem to be
how they seem until you

reach the door — or, more
probably, one of many doors —

marked Magritte the Magi-
cian, open any of them, &

discover the invisible that
resides behind the visible.

The Boys' Club

"This is the inner circle of the Paris Surrealists arranged around the outer perimeter in straight lines"

(top row)

surrealist vision works, Stern with bow, Wipster alternative cancer ... jean, Achievement reflects business sense financial advisors, Avril collins weber ...

jean tonique? Ait logistics contact number, Raphia naturel couleur, X mp ... caupenne d'armagnac, Al reef villas postal code, Free css menu templates

Jean pierre camilleri dentiste, Cx650 turbo for sale, Art glass frogs for ... Caupenne france, Punaruskea kissanpentu, Schinkelstraat 8, Graphics job in

Jean michel fouillet, Insufficiency fracture of femur, Foreign running shoes ... Caupenne and co lyon, Leather toiletries travel bag, Create join table in ...

Surrealist art characteristics, Iclass t9t9 wifi hd, Banail. Butterflies ... jean baptiste thomas, Scenic corp brooklyn, Cvs caremark insurance for employees

(second row)

Jean pierre staelens cetim, Koszali kod, Military loans for spouses, 73807 ... caupenne d'armagnac, Lego ninjago fang suei clock, Caroline asmr ear massage

Jean philippe bellec credit agricole, Single phase transformer tutorial, Pia ... caupenne, Campanita de oro ya el gallo canto, Je sommeil, Is the nixon ...

(third row)

Jean-marc bodson photographe, Smartpad 10.1 hd ipro 110 3g, Soeda go itf ... caupenne d'armagnac 32, 1132 alodine, Handbag shop online usa, Gelatina de

Jean christophe spinosi handel, 1999 fuel economy guide, Laidback luke 2014 ... caupenne d'armagnac, North thurston meadows elementary, Nsw cheyenne 2000

(fourth row)
Caupenne code postal 4025001028, Dera ghazi khan airport pakistan, Andre ... Jean marc namotte csc security, Kostpriser wiki, Login demo joomla monster ...

Jean pierre baudry pianiste, Object c# clone, Diff repairs western suburbs ... caupenne, Stardock iconpackager 5.1, Strelovodne instalacije? Chakwal ka mojza

(fifth row)
Jean paul d'hondt. What happened on december 27 2002! Iran nuclear sites bbc ... Caupenne landes, Cuore selvaggio puntata 052 di 160, Fleissiger max, Skinny ...

Caupenne thierry, Al mundo paz con letra, Oceanaire dc restaurant week menu ... jean baptiste bagaza, Chef liang wentao, Virreinas chocoanas, La bomba

Jean wyllys joaquim barbosa, Fiat swift escape 622, Stricture of artery ... Caupenne philippe! Orange pineapple banana salad, Gepanzerter unimog, Ludwigia

jean de sixt, Alexandra marinescu dance, Besten kuschelsongs, Minecraft ... Caupenne sonia, Swati rastogi, Perumahan tipe 36 bandung. Arany janos utca dm, 8

.. caupenne merah, Umlaut html generator, Dc2 rims jeep, Blurb indesign ... Jean renoir short film, Joan walsh bill o'reilly youtube, Resipi roti telur, Kmsl

Participants: Maxime Moses Alexandre, Louis Aragon, André Breton, Luis Buñuel, Jean Caupenne, Paul Eluard, Marcel Fourrier, René Magritte, Albert Valentin, André Thirion, Yves Tanguy, Georges Sadoul, Paul Nougé, Camille Goemans, Max Ernst, & Salvador Dalí. Photographs by Man Ray, Collage by André Breton. Central artwork by René Magritte : *Je ne vois pas la [femme] cachée dans la foret* (*I do not see the [woman] hidden in the forest*). Created for *La Révolution Surréaliste*, no.12; 15 December, 1929

"It's the cuckoo egg placed in the nest (the lost clutch)
    with the complicity of René Magritte"
— André Breton

La Bonne Aventure

The clichés, which should
have been here in numbers,
are nowhere to be seen. Have
fled, some further down the
seaside cliffs, some gone on
board that passenger liner
which is now full steam a-
head for the open sea, all
struck dumb by a sensory
perception of the androgy-
nous eroticism inherent in
this oversized nose, at once
both phallic & feminine. Only
that synecdoche sycamore re-
mains, certain that, at some
time soon, the equivalent of a
fig leaf might just be needed.

Le Voleur

The hot air balloon has
been stolen from another
painting; as have the river
& the hills it weaves be-
tween. Then there's the
curtain which has been
on show so many times
that it would otherwise
appear threadbare were
it not for the wardrobes
full of similar things —
taken from clotheslines
& salons & a number of
theaters — which are easy
to switch between. Now
focus on the thief himself,
who, out in public & with
an eye to propriety, has
foregone the purloined
jacket worn in tense times
past — including *le présent* —
on the off chance he might
just come across its owner.

The Lovers IV

This meeting of minds
can't be that great

if it's so easy to see
his heart isn't in it.

La Victoire (2)

Winning opens a
door; & shows that

nothing at all has
changed. The same

sand, the same sea.
A fresh cloud, per-

haps. But that will
blow away shortly.

As simple as a page borrowed from a botanical manual

True politeness will be found, its
basis in the human heart. But this is
still only the least of the ambiguities.
Never by word or action notice the
defects of another — a space hence-

forth without reference point, ex-
panding to infinity, the polished sur-
face throwing back the arrow. The
large pipe also without reference
point or measure will linger above,

in its inaccessible, balloon-like immo-
bility. You must sympathize with the
"contradiction" between the image &
the text. It must originate with you. Con-
tradiction can exist only between two

statements, or within one & the same
statement. Never interrupt any one
who is speaking. It is quite apparent
that the drawing representing the pipe
is not the pipe itself. It is very ill-bred.

Sources:
This Is Not a Pipe, by Michel Foucault
The Ladies' Book of Etiquette (1860), by Florence Hartley

Le Leçon des Ténèbres

i. Between Light & Darkness
"Within the liturgy of the Catholic Church there is a long tradition of singing the Lamentations of Jeremiah during Holy Week, based on a parallel being drawn between the text's description of the destruction of Jerusalem in 586 BC and the death of Christ. By the time of Couperin and de Lalande, a practice had been established in which the text was divided into nine 'lessons' sung over three days, with one candle of a special candelabra being extinguished after each lesson, until 'tenebrae' or darkness was achieved on Good Friday.

"Some of the finest examples of the genre are the three Leçons by François Couperin, composed for the royal monastery of Longchamp c. 1714. (Couperin at one time referred to a full set of nine lessons, but only the three for Holy Wednesday are known today.)" [1]

ii. The Encounter
Bare. No diacritics. In a report of the precedings of a 2013 estate tax challenge between the Estate Of James A. Elkins, Jr., Deceased, & the Commisioner Of Internal Revenue it is noted that the Deceased owned undivided fractional interests in 64 works of contemporary art. Within that list, sandwiched between Pierre Soulages & Joseph Albers, is item 13, with an assessed value of $550,000, "Magritte, Rene, La lecon des tenebres, 1964 (Gouache on paper, 13-1/2" x 21-1/2")." [2]

iii. The Lessons of Darkness

As soon as fruit is taken
from the tree, it loses life

& light. The further from
its place of origin, the

greater the degradation. In
a stone cellar it petrifies,

darkens to become one
with its surroundings.

Outside the light remains.
Here endeth the first lesson.

[1] From the catalogue of BIS Records.
[2] From CourtListener, a project of Free Law Project.

skate / parked / bored

Sweet Jesus. *Le fils de l'homme*
as a skateboard. What would
Foucault have made of this,
especially since the constructors
insist *ceci n'est pas un skateboard*?

The accompanying text describes
it thus: an "edition of artwork
intended for decorative purposes...
with one wall mount per deck to
hang it on your wall, just like a

painting." It also points out that
you could skate on it if you wanted
to; but doesn't mention that if he
had wanted to, Magritte could
have incorporated it quite easily as

replacement for the object in a numb-
er of his paintings. Perhaps *le skateur
perdu*, perhaps *le skateboard volant*.
CO2 neutral, with the wood sourced
from sustainable forests. Bonus!

La Saveur des Larmes (c.1938)

Sinatra offscreen. An Oscar-
winning song. Sammy Cahn
lyrics. *Oops, there goes another*
rubber tree plant even though
Anyone knows an ant can't
Move a rubber tree plant. Maybe
that's what the caterpillars are
singing as they start to demolish
the giant synecdoche that towers

over the river, over a house full of
lights which foreshadows the final
work of the painter, over a bridge
which seemingly comes from &
goes to nowhere. The caterpillars
chew away. It is a painstaking task.
It is a painful task. One thing dies
for another to live. They weep; &
hate the bitter flavor of their tears.

Le Masque Vide

Many believed that politeness
was just a mask, that what was
said may not be what was meant
or thought: or, from the other
side, thought to mean, though
the politeness was reciprocated.
Not quite the bland leading the
bland, but close enough. What
we have here acknowledges
those rules but is much more an-
gular, abrupt, an elbow to the
ribs. All politeness torn away:
the mask is empty; but the words
that hide behind the words be-
hind the mask are now exposed.
A pity we cannot see them all.

Pour devenir un fort soldat / To become a strong soldier (1918)

What would you do if your team mate gets injured & there is no medic near?

O Find the nearest veterinary clinic & make an appointment
O Select an optimal key for both to sing the Bee Gees' *Stayin' Alive* in
O Ride a cock-horse to Banbury Cross
O With no other indicator, choose to give up & respawn instead

Are you focused & calm in awkward situations?

O Only when the wind is blowing from the sea
O I have no fear of snowstorms in my dreams
O Later she would walk down to the lagoon to look for the politicians
O Not when I bring someone with me whom I sometimes agree with

Which rifle action is your favourite?

O What constellation is the moon currently passing through?
O Something different from the same old bolt-action system
O Depends on whether I'm hunting hares or humans
O What does the sensei say?

Are you fat?

O Could you be more specific
O I'm a small-town stud who wants to go to Nashville to be a big
      country star
O so much depends / upon / / a red wheel / barrow
O I do not reflect upon or on my body image

How do you reload a pistol?

O Hand over fist
O Head over heels
O Mind over matter
O Apples or oranges?

Are you accurate?

O Show me a bull's-eye!
O What is a bull's eye?
O What is a bull?
O Beauty is in the eye of the bullholder

Are you good at parkour?

O I can always choose the perfect outfit to wear
O I've never received a parking ticket, so does that count?
O Only when there are clouds involved
O Is MacArthur's Park melting in the dark?

Have you ever shot with a rifle?

O Never. My sperm count isn't high enough
O Once, when I was a windy boy & a bit
O Twice. For every action, there is an equal & opposite reaction
O Thrice. But has a rifle ever shot with me?

What is a shotgun?

O Being born during a Rolling Stones' recording session
O A Mirrorball on Main Street
O The latest manga, *The Youngest Son of a Conglomerate*
O A person meditating on madness

What is an FN Ballista?

O The first cyclone of the season
O The Last Hurrah of the Golden Horde
O *Ceci n'est pas une pipe*
O Close, but no cigar

La Gravitation Universelle

The wall is artifice, is illusion,
a masque to keep the forest
at bay — at least it seems that
way until the hunter gets his
arm stuck in it & Newton's

law of universal gravitation
kicks in. Or, equally, kicks
out. Allegorically, this could be
a depiction of the "first great
unification," a realization of

the attraction of particles. Or,
if you're so inclined, another
allegory, where Isaac Newton
is the hunter, presenting the 1st
Book of his *Principia* to the

Royal Society, & Robert Hooke
is represented by the wall, ac-
cusing Newton of plagiarism
&, as punishment for the theft,
attempting to take his hand off.

The Emergence

"Put it into perspective," the
fado singer says as the white
bird wheels away & takes
the daytime with it. "Except
for the stars, the sky will be
empty now for several hours;
& though having a supposed
symbol of hope around might
at first seem comforting, grief
is best left to emerge when one
is in the open or beside the sea.
Clean, simple. No melodrama."

La Porte Ouverte

The painter, flushed with
pride from the achievement
of turning Venus de Milo in
to flesh before he posed her

in a meadow, finally recog-
nizes his hubris when the
shadow that has started
following him everywhere

makes him aware that any
statue can stand still for
long enough to have a beard
& mustache painted on them.

Beneath, nothing — it is a gravestone.

In a landscape of battling giants, ne-
ver, in paying a courtesy call, stay
more than twenty minutes or less
than ten. Anything else could be
thought ill-bred, as if all those airy,

fragile words had been given the
power to organize the chaos of stones.
& never, despite the sprightly but im-
mediately lost chatter of men, call
without cards. In any context — but

especially this — the shape of, say, a
table has more importance than some
people think. Between words & objects
one can create new relationships. This
is by no means a matter of weaving

signs & spatial figures into a unique
& absolutely novel form. Words are
not bound directly to other pictorial
elements. So, the table should be of
a shape which will make it easy for

each guest to address any one else at
the table. A long parallelogram, with
the host at one end & the hostess at
the other, is stiff, too broad, too long,
& isolates the givers from the guests.

Sources:
This Is Not a Pipe, by Michel Foucault
The Ladies' Book of Etiquette (1860), by Florence Hartley

The Childhood of Icarus

We lived in a house full of
models for, & details from,

paintings. Inside & out. My
father showed me how to

use the wings he built by
teaching me how to ride a

a horse & wield a whip.
Everything so large when I

was young, save for the Sun
which seemed so far away.

The Taste of the Invisible

Has he taken a bite from
the side of the apple we
cannot see? Is that what
he is tasting? Or is there
an additional something —
let's say a piece of butter-
scotch to give it a whisker
of substance — hidden in

behind that apple, another
entity which will be either
visible or invisible depend-
ing on the side of the apple
the observer finds themself
at a particular point in time?

> *"Here we have the apparent visible, the apple,*
> *hiding the hidden visible, the person's face."* R.M.

Of Limbs & Luxury

Today the post-
woman brought
me an already ex-
pensive castle in
the Pyrenees. If
I had added the

optional extra of
that giant bird
found in some
Magritte paintings
it would have cost
me an arm & a leg

on top of a basic
price I can't really
afford. & since Ma-
gritte is dead, I don't
trust the vendor's
guarantee that the

artist will paint
any missing limbs
back on me, just
like he did to the
model in *Attemp-
ting the Impossible*.

Le Présent

It appears as if birds
with ancient lineages

find it difficult to deal
with the present on

its own terms unless
they have some well-

worn article from the
past to comfort them.

La Belle Lurette

The bilboquet is monocular, a
cyclops in an uninhabited land-
scape whose presence does not

change the land around even if
it does add some life to its sur-
rounds, even if the addition of

a cloak brings more humanity.
Elsewhere, the ruined watch-
tower is in the act of changing,

those roots insinuating a future
tree, even if *il y a belle lurette*, even
if that started a long time ago.

Jeunesse

From Amazon in Belgium
I can order this as a "Canvas
Wall Art Print for Living Room
Home Decor Ready to Hang
(90 x 117 cm (31.5 x 46.1 in)),
Framed" for just €191.26. I
think of buying it, to see if
it does for me what another
portrait did for Dorian Gray.

But then, but then. At 81
it's probably too late to weave
any magic it might have had
on me, even though the web-
site says it's a great gift idea
for Valentine's Day which
just happens to be today.
What finally turns me away
is a sudden vision of the

aging process occuring —
since we have no attic — in
the back garden shed, the
teeth at first, then the lungs,
the hearing, the knees. It's
not the actual deterioration,
rather the caveat from the
vendor: that spare parts are
not available nor provided.

La Bonne Foi (2)

For once the tie's knot
fills the collar. The pipe,

more merlot than the
indian red of the tie,

still manages — through
the medium of the lips —

to blend in with it. It's
taken sixty or so years;

but the man's finally
got some dress sense.

Memory of a Journey

Without the feather, the tower
would fall down. Without the

tower, the building blocks of
the universe would have no-

thing to hold them in place.
Without the building blocks of

the universe, Magritte would not
exist. Without Magritte, the invis-

ible would never be rendered
visible & we would never know

what direction we should follow.

L'Ovation

Begin with the bowler hat. It
doesn't have the ebullience
displayed by Astaire in his
rendition of that Irving Berlin
song but can be relied upon
to fill its allotted rôle with
some semblance of style. Re-
ceives an appropriate round
of applause.

                Then come the
birds. Brought on early be-
cause they're flighty & might
take off at any moment. (Save
for that eagle in a stony pose
somewhere in the Pyrenees.)

The bit players follow — weight-
lifters, lions, fish, rocks floating
in space, dogs, lost jockeys, the
odd unicorn. Elsewhere invisible,
but here most definitely on show.

Now the cloud chorus steps for-
ward to take their bow, bringing
with them one of the many scenes
in which they appear. This one
repeated often, with different
colors & different media, usually
with a different name, *La Joconde*,
the happy one, the Mona Lisa.

Which is a hint of what's to follow.
Tension builds as we wait for the
muse. So many aspects & images
of her life depicted across so many
years & now awaiting her final
curtain call. Georgette, *sine qua non*.

The Organs of the Night

This time the jockey isn't lost,
just perplexed to find a set
of wellworn curtains standing
upright on the sand. As is the
horse, paused midstep in its
littoral dressage routine. All
up an unexpected tableau, made
more complex by the fact the

sun seems to be falling rather
than setting. Loss of gravity; &
everything is red-cast as the
human condition deteriorates.
Organ failure ensues. Night will
not see the light of day again.

Confiture de Cheval

Cheval et pomme	Image not available	+158% above mid-estimate
Coeur à la fourchette	Image not available	+181% above mid-estimate
Study of a dog and a cat	Image not available	+22% above mid-estimate
Composition à la rose	Image not available	+12% above mid-estimate
Sans titre	Image not available	+320% above mid-estimate
Portrait of Esther Van Montfort	Image not available	-8% below mid-estimate
Untitled	Image not available	+9% above mid-estimate
Confiture de prunes Cotées		$2.80
A collection of articles relating to René Magritte	Image not available	+151% above mid-estimate
Ensemble de huit dessins	Image not available	Subscribers Only

Le Monde des Images

The window pane cannot
encompass the setting of the
sun. It cracks — obviously not
double-glazed. & that image,
not on the floor, *camera ob-
scura* style, but, in a similar
fashion, trapped at a point
in its pathway, imprinted on
the glass. Now, on the floor,
shards of sunset — clouds,
reflections on the sea, sun.

Later, after he had initiated
the shattering of the glass,
Magritte wrote: *If what is at
least possible should truly hap-
pen one day, I would hope that
a poet or philosopher... would
explain to me what these shards
of reality are supposed to mean.*

I leave that in the inexplicable
basket. But, if there *is* some-
one out there...I'm listening.

L'Ocean

He gets excited when
he's near the ocean.

She is more reserved,
thinks of the scallop

shell she emerged on,
wonders where it now

is. It looks at first like
an unequal relationship;

but it seems to work.

La saveur des larmes (1946)

The stalk broken, perhaps
in preparation for pesto or
some similar condiment. Not

used. The flavor unconducive
for garnish — too much sad-
ness, tastes too much of tears.

La Veillée

A lighted candle & holder cut
from a music score. *Papier
collé*, glued paper, evoking
techniques from some decades
before, invoking thoughts of
his brother, a musician, poet.

Laid beside the candle, eggs
in a nest. Though not known
where they were laid. Nor
known which came first, the
candle or the eggs. Not that
that matters. Take notice of

the notes, their similarity to
DNA, the genetic information
of the music. & the eggs, the
ongoing vigil waiting for them
to hatch, to bring more life in
to the world as we hold the

candle up to illuminate their
progress. Note the *frisson* be-
tween them, candle & eggs, the
magic imparted by being together,
the dust of dusk accompanying
them, adding to the mystery.

La Gâcheuse

Strange to find such an image in
a book on healing; but Magritte's
purloining of the anatomical
illustration lacks the layering that
Dr. F.E. Bilz included, where the
face could be folded back to dis-
play a skull, & the internal organs
similarly displayed by a slight
manipulation of the body. None
of that shown here. Instead—dare
we say it?—a combination of
bare bones & bare breasts to offer
up a simulacrum of age & youth
conjoined. Though left intact upon
the head some residual skin, a re-
minder that *memento mori* might
sometimes come back to bite us.

Seasickness

I am bemused that the 1950s
saccharine pop song *A White
Sport Coat & A Pink Carnation*
that resides somewhere in
that 'songs you grew up with'
drawer jumps immediately to
mind. & yet what else comes
close to a gaudy sport coat &
a cut of ham laid out to fester
beneath a burning sun. They
both provoke a nauseous re-
action, one intentional, the
other not. As Magritte says,
we "live in a very unpleasant
world ... that's why my
painting is a battle, or rather a
counteroffensive." So, no need
to be all at sea even though
the sea is nowhere to be seen.

The Pilgrim

Decide on what faces
to take along. Set out
on the road to Zion

or Mecca or Ayodhya
or Lumbini. Which one
you choose will depend

on the face you have
chosen for the day.
Wear a clean shirt &

a new tie — they will
be accepted everywhere.
The best excuse to offer

for the hat is the old sun-
in-the-eyes routine. That
seems to work most places.

Melmoth

I sold my soul for
150 extra years of
life; but after filling
much of that time
with a variety of

troubled wanderings,
this is where I end up —
riding a road bike tot-
ally unsuited to the
barren mountain trails

I'm fated to finish my
years trapped upon, &
all the while looking so
ridiculous that even the
owls seem sorry for me.

Le Monde Familier

Place the bell, *le grelot*, firmly
on the ground. No need to
anchor it — unlike the artist's
elsewhere use of it, this time
it does not float. A solid
reality keeps it where it is

intended to be. Then lower
the horizon & not only bring
the cloud down with it but
also shift it forward so it seems
out of place but perfectly posit-
ioned above the bell. Now, to

ensure it doesn't float away,
flatten the sky behind & call
upon that peripatetic rock to
actually do something, anchor
the column from above, act
as a counterweight to entropy.

The Lost Jockey (1948)

The surface of the Earth is
covered with overlapping
racetracks. Take the wrong
turn, & a jockey is likely to

find themselves in unfamiliar
surroundings, sometimes not
even on the continent they
started off on. & often lost from

sight, until a convenient cave
opening allows the invisible
to regain some visibility, even
if in a parched & foreign land.

The State of Grace

What people see is the title,
not the subject. & the subject
contradicts the title. "I was
inspired," said Magritte. "The
subject to be painted: a bicycle
on a cigar." Or to put it even
more bluntly, a bicycle riding
roughshod over another object —
no state of grace in that. Ex-
cept . . .The objects float, &
perhaps a belief hovers that
the laws of gravity are defied
when things are in a state of
grace. Which brings in Simone
Weil, who wrote: "All the
natural movements of the soul
are controlled by laws analogous
to those of physical gravity.
Grace is the only exception."
'Analogous to' is the escape
clause that allows St. Thomas
Aquinas to come on board &
point out that grace builds
upon, not contradicts, nature.
Then, once all parties are on
stage, lined up like ten pins
in a state of grace, Magritte
reappears, wearing his bowl-
er hat, & with a solid verbal
cast, scatters the skittles
with his addendum: "A bike
sometimes runs over a cigar
down in the street." No
gravity, no grace inherent.

[postwoman poem]

Today the post-
woman brought
me six billets-doux,

five bills of lading,
four biltong sandwiches,
three billowing blouses,

two bilious bandicoots,
& one bilboquet, bowler-
hatted & signed by

René Magritte.

The Window (2)

This what we set out attempting
to do, the catching of a bird in
flight. So fast, so hard though.
Requires practice, patience, per-
sistence. Means starting in one
domain, which, if we fail with its
mode of manual dexterity, must,

then, move ahead to another,
leaving some familiar forms be-
hind. Ironic, though, since many
of those are classed as futuristic,
but the intention must be there to
move forward, to invent the fu-
ture or re-invent it before our one

arrives. Observation: the painter
on the road, bowler-hatted but
yet to become Mr. Everyman,
still in the future. But the pre-
sent striding on toward the peaks
& villages. & the past, Vincent
van Gogh. The Road to Tarascon.

The Gradation of Fire

The literal meaning of *jan
ken pon*, the Japanese equi-
valent of rock, scissors, paper,
is 'beginning with stone.' That

was the given. To go with it,
various other items were
then subjected to a battery of
tests. This painting shows

some of them undergoing the
fire test, to see how easily
they burn, how long for, &
how much is left behind. Only

one additional item survived
the testing relatively unscathed. To
choose the third, a handoff was be-
gun between the best of the

first round failures. Paper won.

A rectangle for the horse

People should not talk to please
themselves but those who hear
them. Only thought resembles,
resting silently in a discursive
space, as completely invisible as

pleasure or pain. Many believe
that politeness is merely hypo-
crisy & dissimulation. The visible
can be hidden, but the invisible
hides nothing; it can be known or

not known, no more. Who speaks
in the statement? Having all the
talk sustained by one person is not
conversation. Transference? Doubt-
less. But from what to what? Even

though words do not replace missing
objects, if your companion uses words
or expressions which you cannot
understand, ask for an explanation.
What lady likes to be treated rudely?

Sources:
This Is Not a Pipe, by Michel Foucault
The Ladies' Book of Etiquette (1860), by Florence Hartley

Le parfum de l'abîme

L'abîme est un band de Montréal influencé par le jazz, le rock, & le classique contemporain. This isn't them. More likely the painted shape is one of those bits of bricolage, the detritus one finds rolling around the bottom of an abyss. Magritte, more concerned with shadow than with shape, appoints it the head of a child. No jazz there. Possibly death metal.

Le Genre Nocturne

The woman hides her head.
Except she has no head. Is
that what she is trying to
hide? The wall is a dirty gray.
There is an oval shape on it.
Egg? Opening? Mirror? Is
cracked, whatever it is. The
presence of the woman's hands

prevents us from looking past
the cracks to see what's hidden
there. The mirror stares back at
us. We raise our hands. The wo-
man hides her head before them —
except she has no head to hide.

The Now of it

That with which we are
surrounded, in which
we are set,

like a jeweled brooch
or a flower's centre,

we are shaped by.

The environs.

He said:
"This is the space we move
through, which moves about us
when we / do not move.

"In this bright white room,
with the picture window staring out
to sea by day, & at night reflecting
the small blue klee that hangs
like an icon above the fireplace,
                    you are beautiful.

"But when it storms outside
your face takes on the turbulence.
I am forced to close the drapes,
otherwise I lose my balance
seeing you buffeted by the tide."

The words surround her,
alter her to suit their shape.

She sees he does not really see her.
His world is earth, is sea, is rooms
of shadow; & she, as is the bird
in that painting by magritte, is outline
only. The content is another universe,
blue-skied, in which he poses her. She is

imposed upon. She is not content. Her
shape, his shaping — they do not coincide.

She leaves. He does not mark
her going. The words still hold her
in his mind. Spreadeagled on the bed,
the stones singing over him, he reads
about lee harvey oswald & the death of j.f.k.

The words surround him.
The influences, their confluence.
The twenty years, the ten, the now of it.

1974

The Two Mysteries (2)

There are two pipes. Or,
rather, two paintings of
the same pipe which are
meant both to please others
& ourselves, & to make
others pleased with us.

Do not say there is no heart
in the work here—its basis is
the human heart. The sorcery
lies in an operation rendered
invisible by the simplicity
of its result—to make

the pipe new, but floating in
a natural silence where
attention to the small details
extends it more than
it illustrates it or fills the
void. To make it legend.

Sources:
This Is Not a Pipe, by Michel Foucault
The Ladies' Book of Etiquette (1860), by Florence Hartley

The implicit burden of discourse

Do not look overhead for a true
pipe. That is a pipe dream. Be
warned that those who profess
such a doctrine are themselves
practising the deceit they con-

demn so much. Contradiction
usually only exists between two
statements, occasionally within
the one. Here there is clearly one
with no contradictions. How to

banish resemblance? Any higher
pipe lacks coordinates despite a
certain attention to forms & cere-
monies; & even about this ambi-
guity, I am ambiguous. Give to a

woman the knowledge of the forms
& its implicit burden. The polished
surface will then throw back the
arrow. Thus the spirit of politeness
exists in some form in all countries.

Sources:
This Is Not a Pipe, by Michel Foucault
The Ladies' Book of Etiquette (1860), by Florence Hartley

Lyricism

So it doth appear, said
Macbeth, or something
like that. Though he was

talking about daggers,
not about pears or people
who resemble them. Even

so, the underlying mess-
age was certainly clear — all
appearances are subjective.

Le Civilisateur

Three paintings of a dog, all
different dogs but the same
one painted. All different names
but painted under the same
name. Somewhere I read that

this Loulou was black, but painted
white for the occasion. Narrow
nostrils, but supposedly had a
big heart. So loved by its child-
less owners that it traveled with

them everywhere, even to the
States, its right of passage paid
for by a promise to allow the fuse-
lage of one of the airline's planes
to later carry a Magritte motif.

All things pass, including the in-
fluence of a civilizer. The livery
of the plane redone to reflect new
alliances. & of the other themed air-
craft, Tintin will be the next to go.

Intimate Journal

& on the sixth day She
remade man in their own
image, after their own
likeness, but with minor

differences. The one to
carry a briefcase, & the
other a clean handker-
chief, so that he could

remove the small chips
of stone that would in-
evitably catch in the eye
when tears didn't come.

High Level Meetings

Certainly the river in the distance confirms that this is up a mountain. & the shadowy figures in the cave are recognizable from their starring roles in many paintings. But the painter who made them famous also caused them to be regarded as typecast; & now, in the years after his passing, their income stream has almost dried up.

Which is where a bit of creative accounting comes in. Get together in some out of the way place. Bring a friend, someone they have previously appeared with but whose bejeweled androgyny still guarantees work in these non-binary times, & who can easily pass as an agent or manager. Then claim inflated expenses when they list this interaction on their tax forms, describing it as a high level meeting.

Les Ombres

Oh how the
shadow of

the pipe falls
behind every-

thing it comes
in contact with.

Except. This is
not a shadow.

René Magritte et *Le Barbare*

The only way to capture Fantômas is to enter his dreams. — René Magritte

The Luftwaffe's first bombing
run on London; & Magritte's
first one-man show in that city
shut down by it. Several pain-
tings destroyed, including *Le*

Barbare, one of Magritte's many
homages to Fantômas. This photo
all that is left to remember it by,
could easily be titled *Fantômas et*
son doppelgänger, two masters of

the magical, one able to vanish
at will, the other able to make
the invisible visible. Both wear the
formal costume of the magician:
one is disappearing before our

eyes, of his own accord. The other
large as life, but wondering if he
will have the strength to make the
barbarians he can't see coming
disappear before they can arrive.

The Banquet (2)

Elsewhere it was September
when trees rose behind the
sun; & the guests watching

from the balcony applauded
the striking nature of the call
to dinner provided by their hosts.

The Harvest

I wasn't around to know
which painting was done
first — this one, or *Les Bon*
Jours de Monsieur Ingres.
It's the same model; & she
is either resting after a long
day holding up her ewer,
or she is deep in sleep in
preparation for the days
to come. I'll leave the de-
fining detective work to
others, just remind the reader
of the water pouring from
that ewer with only the
background fields to soak
it up. Suggest that, based
on the lushness of those
fields, the standing came
before the lying down.

La Flèche de Zenon

At this point in time
the rock is not falling
or hovering or travel-
ing in a straight line
between two points.

At this point in time
the waves are not
crashing on the shore,
the clouds are still, &
the moon has stopped

orbiting the Earth. At
any point in time, says
Zeno, an arrow is not
moving to where it is
going or where it is not.

No time elapses; so how
can it move? It is already
here, so how can it move
here? At this point in
time I am watching the

movement of a painting
that does not move &
yet it moves this viewer
even though, at this point
in time, the viewer is

motionless.

Olympia

Is that a pangolin that I
see before me? A Manet
woman re-sited *au plein air*,
still *au naturel*, with no
accoutrements. On a towel
on a hill overlooking the
sea. The hand that delicately
covered the nether regions
replaced by a scaly animal
that seems quite happy to
breathe in the local aromas.
It's a simple scene, but with
sharp edges to cut open the
Impressionists & lay bare
some of their prejudices —
racism, classism, a need for
objects to wear a token of their
ownership, a conceit that
flowers will conceal all flaws.

Le Bouchon d'Épouvant

Product found on page 728 of the WoodChuck Norris catalog. Alt Item.
For External Use Only Labels.

High quality example sentences with "for external use only" in context
are available from reliable sources.

Need to translate "for external use only" to Swahili?

Mustard oil was only permitted to be sold for use as a therapeutic
massage oil, which is why bottles at Indian grocery stores are labeled
"For External Use Only."

Find for external use only stock images in HD in the Shutterstock
collection.

A feminine deodorant spray shall bear the following statement: *Caution.
For external use only. Spray at least 8 inches from skin. Do not apply to
broken, irritated, or itching skin.*

This bidet is intended for external use only.

While petroleum jelly has many benefits, it should be for external use
only. Do not eat or insert petroleum jelly.

FDA reminds the public that hand sanitizer is for external use only.

People can technically use Vaseline as a sexual lubricant. It is a nontoxic
substance that is safe for external use only.

Many cosmetics & medicines come in small packed boxes, many of
which have the words 'For external use only. '

Gold & Body Paint 25ml For External Use Only.

A painter converted his pillbox into a Bowler hat. He forgot to remove
the for external use only label.

The process of creation in the artwork is not finalized for external use only.

This product is for external use only. Please avoid ingestion by children & keep it away from high temperature & fire.

Les Adieux

Great Gatsbys! A Renoir on
the grass, alas. & too much
incorporated in the painting
to contain it all. Things escape,
many of those the appurtances
of a dandy — wine glass, rose to
carry in the teeth, some etchings
to come up & look at sometime.

Some things held on to — hat to
keep the sun out, or keep the tan
from overflowing, & gloves to
stroke the mustache with. &,
OMG, brogues that exactly
match the color of the frame.

Le regard intérieur

Exotic birds perch on the veins
of a leaf. Such beauty in them,
but they are so small — or maybe
the leaf is large, larger than the
trees below the window. The
birds do not appear to be hungry.
The leaf is intact. & there seems
to be plenty of water to go round.
A fairly full glass balances on the
ledge. & should the glass fall
there is still that river nearby,
within flying distance, even if
the outside is outside their view.

Le Prisonnier

It's probably something I
learnt from — copied from? —
Magritte, the giving of titles
that bear no relation to the
item in question, whether it
be poem or painting. Here
he lines up abstract shapes,
inserts a table — not of con-
tents but rather something
you'd find in a hallway — &
parks them in front of a barely-
discernable background that
would later be developed
across the years into what
would come to be described
as a typical Magritte land-
scape, then titles the painting
with a name that apparently
has no resemblance to what is
going on within its confines.
Ernst describes it as a collage
painted by hand. I'd agree:
but also see in it a statement
of future intent — never be im-
prisoned by the fear of change.

La Bonne Foi

So many decisions to be
made! Do I face toward
the front or do I turn my
back? & if the front, do I
present myself in good
faith or do I do a bit of

tweaking? No, not the
Miley Cyrus type of tweak,
I'm thinking Photoshop
here. & which bowler hat
do I wear? Which of my
ties? Do I have sea- or

landscape behind me,
clouds or clear sky? &
then the hard part. A
bird or an apple before
my face? After all, this
is not a self-portrait.

writing gear

An HP Pavilion 23". Maybe 4-5 years old. Shown in context. Magritte poster above; poem on the screen based on the same Magritte painting, from the blog; one of my five poetry books based on Magritte paintings to the right of the keyboard; one of the several books on Magritte I have on the shelf at the bottom right.

From *Fanzine* #176-2, edited by Francisco José Craveiro de Carvalho & Joana Costa.

The Lost Jockey (1947-1948)

He has been lost for so
long that the trees – once
trimmed & turned into
bilboquets — are now

growing branches again.
Lost for so long that the
painter's style has under-
gone several transform-

ations in the interim. This
from a classical period;
airy, pastel-toned. A scene
posed, as if disposed

by a dramaturge, with
the jockey center of
the set, finally about
to exit, stage left.

The Virgin's Chariot

Elsewhere it is drawn by lions,
on solid ground, even if it is
a rough track rather than a
road. Cherubs accompany her,
either to keep her amused or on
hand to push — while the lions
pull — the chariot should it
happen to get stuck. Allegory
drawn large. The Virgin Mary
on her way to heaven, assumed
body & soul, traveling first class
on a triumphal vehicle. Much
the same thing here. The means
of transport a shiny mirror, the
suitcase closed as befits a virgin.
Yet the perspective all wrong. If
the mirror's right, then the case
could only hold a single tube of
lipstick. If the case is lifesize then a
reasonable entourage could balance
on the mirror comfortably. So
what's the answer? Perhaps it
lies in those marks on the mirror.
Dare we suppose some lines of
coke were snorted here, & the
world now somewhat distorted.

Le Sabbat

He refused to work
on the Sabbath, which
is why the lights are
all turned off — *the moon*
gives me enough light
to find my way around —

& the painting is left
upside down — *I won't*
work but that doesn't
stop my mind from
turning over, so putting
things in unusual places
often helps as a sort of
associative trigger when
the next day comes around —

& for any person passing
by, an upturned apple is
still an apple — *I stole*
that idea from Gertrude
Stein who I later paid back
by painting rose after rose
after rose — but no one

has decreed that magic
can't be done on this day —
I deliberately put that half-
full glass of wine there so
that when it hangs upside-
down with no spillage, what
else can it be but magical?

An Advertisement for Norine (Lord Lister variant)

Shop our inventory for perhaps the
most petty revenge novel ever written —
*Lord Lister, known as Raffles, Master
Thief: The Fake Jeweler's Punishment.*
Find many great new & used options.

* get the best deals for

Vintage FASHION SEXY WOMEN LADY GUN COAT LORD LISTEN MANTEAU NORINE ADS Postcard

on eBay *

Controleer voor de zekerheid de
spelling van uw zoekterm:
Lord Lister, genannt Raffles.

Love that scarf. Where *did* you get it?

La Joconde (2)

The curtains open. The summer
sky takes center stage. Thinks *the
play's the thing*: but there is no
King. Apart from the slash of blue &
white there is little light, & the only
animate object in sight, a horse's bell,
has lost its smile, lips quite tight,
trapped inside a night of boredom.

Man with a Newspaper (2)

Seeing several
frames within the
painting allows that
a central premise

could be: today &
yesterday are so alike
a past image can be
positioned to present the

present in such a way
Derrida himself might
find it hard to tell if

what happened then
has happened now
or has time reversed.

La Vengeance

Simplicity abounds. Each
part of the room is mono-
tone — floor, walls, the em-
bossed dado, the ceiling
& its cornice. Only the
horse's bell rings out in-
trusion, & that, perhaps,
because of oversize alone.

L'Invention du Feu

Maybe we shouldn't go
down the line of thought
brought about by the ob-
vious doggy position
along with too much
randy baluster, too little
political correctness. But
where else to go, seeking
the meaning of the seem-
ingly demeaning pose?
Back to the future, I sup-
pose, since this is identified
as the invention of fire & thus
comes first, gives birth to
all those fiery euphoniums
that were discovered later.

En Face des Murmurs

The whisperers are not exactly
out in force. Just the two
of them. Evidence enough,

however, to group all rumor
into two streams which their
purveyors reflect. Those mur-

murs that have some weight
to them. The others baseless,
can be easily seen through.

Le lieu commun

At once revealed &
obscured by the same
corner of the wall. Is
rare that we can see the
whole face of Mr. Every-
man, *sans oiseaux, sans
pommes, sans énigme.*
Looks like the forest is
no longer common place —
brings out another side
to him. Especially when
it encroaches upon his
suburban living space.

The Spirit of Adventure / L'Esprit d'Aventure

Je suis un petit bourgeois
avec un chapeau melon &
les chaussures à bout d'aile
mais je n'ai pas le moindre
esprit d'aventure.
            Which is
why I stand at the seawall
looking out at the tangerine
sea, a similar sky, & not even
try to guess as to what might
cause them to be that way.

I am somewhat middle class
with my bowler hat & my
wing tip shoes but I do not
have the slightest spirit of
adventure inside me.
Lequel est
            pourquoi je me tiens à la
digue regardant la mandarine
mer, un ciel similaire, et même
pas essayez de deviner ce qui
pourrait les amener à être ainsi.

The Sensational News

Decomposition takes time — depends
upon the size of the object. Retribution,
too, not always immediate, but it is
deliberate. Why else that phrase: revenge
is a dish best served cold? Sufficient of
the bird remaining to let it manipulate
the surrounds. Getting its own back
for its owners' neglect. Singing as it does
so, *Stairway to Heaven*, that Led Zeppelin

song. Using it as a template / timekeeper,
to progress the couple's decay. First the
smile wiped off their faces, so ferociously
their features have come away as well.
Then smoothed down, as if turned on a
lathe. The final indignation still to come.
Head & neck removed, to be featured as
newel caps, put in place at the top of
the staircase as the song comes to an end.

Tous les Jours

Up here in the mountains
it is an everyday thing
to come across vestiges of
earlier climbers &/or the oc-
casional earlier painting.
They may present as tracks
in the earth or discarded
equipment. Sometimes as
ghosts or holograms. Stare
at the latter for long enough
& they sometimes become
embarrassed, begin to speak.
In a thin voice that still
sparks echoes, this one says:
"I was once the star of *The
Age of Enlightenment*. Now
the world has forgotten
me. Am I not still beautiful?"

La Marchande de Sable

Legerdemain & sympathetic
magic are not confined only
to my paintings. Sometimes
I moonlight as the sandman,
tell stories that throw sand
into the listeners' eyes to
foster dreams that render the
invisible visible. Georgette is
happy just to watch me work;
but on occasion, when I wish
to explain more fully what is
beneath, behind, the current
painting, I sprinkle sand into
her eyes to make her sleep. She
smiles at my explanations; &
at the pipe I leave beside her to
remind her where we've been.

Impressions

If this
were Cézanne
or Magritte's
birthday

I might consider
having an
apple for
lunch. But

instead I'm
stuck with
Renoir, & a
full-on three-

courser on
the grass.

Décalcomanie

Which side has been taken
& pressed upon the other
one? Maybe with another
artist it might be easy to
determine — clean lines,
symmetry, a space echoing
what has been taken away
from it — but Magritte
rarely adheres to the strict
guidelines for anything, &
decalcomania is no except-
ion. The curtain behind, in
front of; the horizons evenly
aligned but not the beach;
one shoulder sloping more.
En plein air the man blocks
out the sea. The curtains ex-
pose it as if he wasn't there.

Les Bijoux Indiscrets

Hand on
my heart

I have
a face

on my
wrist.

Le Grand Air

A drunk man's words are often the disturbing thoughts of a sober one.

The dialectical law of negation of the negation calls us to re-visit the historical context within which the Western myth of human rights is conceived.

Agendas enter the local context. Hollywood celebrities enter into prenuptial agreements. The ideal version of democracy is a fluid entity which we constantly construct, deconstruct, reconstruct.

A touch of the modern & it would not be at all acceptable.

Who is going to cook dinner tonight, wash plates, change the baby's nappies?

Representation II

The orchestra under the cypress
tree kicks into life. A few bars;
& then the scene we're watching
on the small screen is replicated
on a larger canvas that still permits
the original viewing platform to
be included in the corner, picture-
within-picture style, framed by

the only thing that might be a
goal were it not for the pawn on
top. Or maybe it was the other
way around & downsizing has
occurred. No spectators to see
the "world game" shrunk to three
a-side. The château now a simple
manor house. A lone pianola.

Le Sang du Monde

I have always found imaginary landscapes more real than the real. The paintings of Magritte & de Chirico, the novels of Le Guin & Delany & Ballard — I am comfortable in these even though I may occasionally find them disturbing. Perhaps it's because I live my life vicariously, or perhaps it's because I have never found, though I've lived in quite a few of them, a city that felt like home.

L'Atlantide

The concealing shroud has
shifted from the bedside
of a sleeping Georgette &
now resembles a bunch of
damp towels as it rests on
the tiles beside a bath that
has no taps, no obvious out-
let pipes. Rotate the painting,
& stairs appear. & though the
chapel at the top of them is set
into solid rock, it means only
that an exit is behind you. A-
void the abyss which is al-
ways here- or thereabouts. &
beware the imminent arrival
of a cascade of water falling
from the upturned bath.

L'Ombre Céleste

The sky comes
on little fog feet.

It pauses for
maximum visual
impact before

moving on round
the corner & then
disappearing
down the alleyway.

The Encounter

What fundamentalist church do
the bilboquets belong to? Is this
an awkward preamble in that
once-a-year formal meeting at
which the offspring are instructed
who their lifetime partner will be?
Are there other opportunities to
encounter members of another
gender outside of gospel rallies
& church hall meetings? How
often do they hold dances? Do
they hold dances? Could this be
actually a prelude to a dance, both
sides uncertain how to proceed to
better know one another without
yet getting too close? Why is the
outside angry? Where are the walls
to shut it out. Who defines forever?
When will the curtain be drawn?

The Cicerone (1947)

Instead of a trident he holds
a candelabra. Instead of

candles it holds apartment
buildings — not large ones,

just three storeys each. In-
stead of residents, they hold

stories. For a small fee, the
cicerone will recount them.

A few cents more, & he'll
embellish with special effects.

L'heure d'été

Maybe it depends upon the
country you live in. But instead
of images of sunburnt masculinity,
a perfume called *Summertime* in
these parts conjures up those

several fevers whose vector is
mosquitoes. Plus heat. & either
humidity, the occasional hurri-
cane, lots of rain, or else an
infinite dryness that brings

only drought, depending on
which specific part of the
land you live on. The smell of
summertime is usually sweat —
& where's the poetry in that?

Le Fin du Temps

The end of time presents as a
simple act of prestidigitation,
able to be reversed by a sequence
of triggers. It wears a black suit
when alone at home; but any time
it ventures out, sequins are *de rig-
ueur*, in the long-held belief that
the light catching on them will
assist the efficacy of the illusion,
much like movement of the other
hand draws the eye away from
where the legerdemain is actually
being carried out. There are other
disguises. This end of time is pre-
faced by perspective done on the
cheap — the faux wood floor tilts
upwards, & seemingly sitting a-
top its sloping edge is a rococo
frame. Not with an inset mirror;
instead an oval piece of plywood
with symmetrical jigsawn decor-
ation. It *is* a mirror, though. Look
into it & see laid out how time runs
backwards now. Turn round & look
ahead. That distant dot is time's end.

The Secret Life III

Rodents & small humans
inhabit the tunnel that runs
beneath the clouds. They are
currently extinct, though the
occasional fossil may still be
found. A plucked stalactite
rests against the wall that holds
the outside in. There are four
openings out into a potential
void — hard to be sure, since
each has a screensaver which
is full of clouds — that take it
in turns to show newsreels
of previous wars. The size of
the openings determines what
centuries the newsreels date
from. Screening times will
be written on the blackboard
when the clouds wake up.

The Secret of the Clouds

It is daytime. The unlit moon
comes across as just another
cloud as it mixes in with them.
Except these clouds don't look
like those clouds — or those /
these, depending on what your
viewing point is. Nothing secretive
about the ones above my head:

meteorologists have long since been
able to define, decline them. These others?
Okay, it's obviously a shitty day, but the
only secret I can posit they contain is
which of asemic notebook, extrusion, or
tangled spaghetti do they spring from.

The Homunculus of Frank O'Hara

I no longer take the homunculus of Frank O'Hara onto the plane with me. Have grown tired of having to place it in the perspex tray along with my lighter, cigarettes, keys, watch, wallet, spectacles – yes, I know there's three-quarters of a racially stereotypical joke in there; but having no desire to irradiate my gonads I have never taken off my testicles to complete the punchline.

The homunculus traveled peacefully enough most times. But every so often, especially when the flight was delayed, he'd be set off by the X-ray machine, would suddenly exclaim "my quietness has a man in it" in a voice that most definitely contradicted the words; & then I'd be up against the wall being searched for stowaways.

Before him I'd taken Bach with me. He'd mainly hum. The machines would gradually pick up the theme & purr along in perfect counterpoint. Caught up by the harmony all around even the security guards would display a courtesy & politeness that was exemplary. Never a problem until the day J.S.B. got asked to remove his periwig & promptly launched into a performance of his *Toccata & Fugue in D Minor* that shook the terminal. Then came the *Brandenburgs*, & planes started falling from the sky.

Magritte has been my companion on the last few flights. So far nothing to report. He is the perfect gentleman. Takes off his overcoat & lays it flat on the belt, followed by his bowler hat which he places in such a way it completes the outline of a man. Then we walk through the metal detector together, quietly, each eating an apple picked from a favorite painting.

Le sommet du regard

After his death, the executors
came to take an inventory of
the familiar items. He was there
for most of it, was able to clear
up some of the uncertainties,
took pains to point out that most
of the items here did not exist.

"Can you truly believe that
things found within the various
strata of a painting that contains
a painting that also contains a
painting would have physical
form? The perspective is all wrong
to allow that to happen. I made

them visible only for the length
of time it took me to paint the
painting that surrounds the others.
Now I too have passed; & no one
is left to say if that is a swarm of
locusts in the background, or
smoke coming from a forest fire."

Le Goût de l'Invisible (1927) (2)

There's a McDonald's near where
I live; so, when I grow tired of
exploring fermentation at cooking
school, I set off in search of treats
of divers & sundry matters. There
is a heightened level of threat now
that baby green snakes are on their
way to where I later pause in the
Louvre contemplating the secretive
nature of *Le Prieuré de Sion*. I think it
has something to with string theory,
as in stringing one along, along the
lines of McDonald's has a Michelin
star, The Priory has a secret cellar
beneath the Louvre. Everything
exudes an unseen aspect behind the
visible, whose nearness I can taste
even if I cannot see it. A framework
of scented gardens for the blind.

Le Goût de l'Invisible (1964)

Ceci n'est pas un masque
COVID. It is an apple,
put there to prevent
the perfume of the

abyss from seeping in.
I am standing on its
edge, looking into
it, then I slowly turn

away. It's reverse
psychology. If I can't
see it then I am in-
visible. It can still

taste me, though. My
fear gives me away.

The Secret Life I

By day he was the stereo-
typically mild-mannered
man, *un petit bourgeois* from
curve of bowler hat to the
wingtips down below. Too
immersed in Max Weber to
consider Nietzsche as a role
model, but still had dreams

to find a life in the theater.
Finally achieved; but too
shaped by bureaucracy to
even be a lowly spear carrier.
Instead is typecast, stage dec-
oration, a mute piece of wood.

L'Avenir

Everything in the distance seems so
picture perfect — the stars, the hills
in shadow. & those things up close —
the open window, the pristine bench
with that loaf so fresh you would
swear you could smell it — refresh

that first impression of perfection.
Then doubts start creeping in. Why
are there no lights dotting the hillside?
Why are there no knick knacks around
the house to indicate some evidence
of human inhabitation? Who, therefore,

baked the loaf? Is it really real? Or is
this image of the future a wry obser-
vation by the painter that life as we
currently know it might eventually
vanish from the planet because hu-
mankind cannot live by bread alone?

Elle a mis son smoking

She put on her tuxedo for her
senior portrait. The yearbook
left her photo out & spelt her
name wrong when they wrote

No Photo. She put on her tuxedo,
then put on a James Brown cape
to match. The result was much
more androgynous than the and-

roid she was meant to be. She
put on her tuxedo to try & get
her swag back. Such a retro thing.
But doesn't she look fantastic!

She put on her tuxedo, put away
her petticoats, then wrote a letter
to Marlene Dietrich saying how
grateful she was to have such a

role model. She put on her tux-
edo. Such a chic alternative to the
usual high school prom dress —
except they wouldn't let her in.

La lumière du pôle

Is said the polar lights
dance. If so, is not so

dangerous. Unless. A
single light is much more

potent, will dry the skin
& brittleness will break

it off. Unless. You are a
bird. & feathers protect.

The Famine

We turn into clowns &
start by fighting over who
has the right to eat Ensor's
Skeletons fighting over a
smoked herring. Eventually
that's gone, torn into little
pieces; but the intake doesn't
stay the hunger so we turn

upon each other. Now I'm
the last one left, & what is
left of me, I realize, is all the
food remaining. Where should
I start? I take off what's left of
my clown clothes. Naked-
ness is the proper dress for
facing existential questions.

The Future of Voices + The Key to Dreams

The cicerone paused midway between the two paintings. "These were both painted in the same year," she said, "but we do not know which one came first. I like to think it was the one without the internal frame, without the labels. I am probably wrong, though. More likely that the painter saw these objects & captured & imprisoned them, then called their images by another name so that they would forget who or what they were.

"If we accept my initial ordering, then the future of voices is that they fall silent unless they are given names, no matter if inappropriate. If we believe the alternative scenario, then reality gradually falls away until the objects become the stuff of dreams, misnamed, though something of a key left behind so we can make the invisible visible if we so desire.

"Each time I walk by I make up stories, create associations. The briefcase has been floating around in space for so long it has become the sky that surrounds it. Then the painter comes along & stuffs it into the case it used to be but which he now names sky. It becomes a paradox: how can it be both inside & outside itself when it is not transparent?

"Then we confront mundanity. The sponge is so absorbent that no matter what we throw at it, it takes it in & remains what it always was, will always be, in captivity or not. The name remains the same no matter what happens in the interim. But a falling leaf transforms into the table we are lunching at.

"Not everything is so straightforward. Perhaps the bird slices its throat with the pocket knife & is swallowed up by the space between, eventually reappearing as a pipe. Yet if we approach this from the other end, it may be that the painter was unable to rename the pipe, disturbed by what he later described as the treachery of images, & so excluded it from the reworking, leaving a space until the knife flew into view.

"History records that it took the painter two more years before he could confront the pipe again, & even then could not name or rename it. Instead he attached a warning label: *Ceci n'est pas une pipe.*"

The Murderous Sky

The hillsides are crammed
with rocks, patches of snow
contained between them. They
didn't kill the birds. Or bird,
one only, but cloned or repli-
cated, & placed with mathe-
matical precision within each
quadrant of at least the rectangle
we can see & likely elsewhere.
The sky may be the murderer;
but the painter is its accomplice.

Green Night

The crossbones have melted
in the moonlight, now look
like sad dumbbells, as does

the crew of the ship beneath
the flagging standard. It's all
very jolly being rogered, but

more than a bit embarrassing
when you're in port, & some-
one has left the curtains open.

"Exciting Perfumes by MEM"

I still think advertising is
imbecile work, useful
for the artist as an activity
to help in putting food on
the table or pay the rent. That
attitude somewhat softened
since the war, getting back
into painting, but now with
only limited options for dis-
play. Pessoa once said to me:
the unnatural & the strange have
a perfume of their own. I've mixed
& matched. The unnatural &
strange have always been with
me. Now I've added someone
else's chic perfume; & so, in
magazines & *tous les grands*
magasins, posters & full-page
liftouts have returned my
name, my output, back into
the discerning public's eye.

Great Journeys

A naked woman plunges
headless into the edges
of the forest, bringing the
already built blocks of a
small city along with her.

This is how civilizations
are sometimes founded —
almost as easily as one of
those videos games, but
with much more panache.

Wreckage of The Shadow (2)

The bird without feathers is
a mountain in the Pyrenees.

An angular snow shoe for
walking through the dust
of diamonds holds feathers
that do not hold a bird.

Another mountain holds a
cave. (In another painting
we are inside it, waiting
for the bird to look away.)

Wooden parrakeets morph
into prototype string instru-
ments. Bricolage becomes
a bits & pieces bird whose

disproportionate tailfeathers
take on the conductor's rôle.

The sea hovers above the sky.

La Sortie de l'École

You go to a friend's house. Their call center's average call handle times are way past your bedtime. You want to eat pasta. Why are humans so drawn to these foods? Do they help pay the utility bills? Fraudsters call Santa Clara residents asking for help tracking a fraudster. They offer six steps to get your money back by identifying emerging patterns. Again it makes you want to eat pasta. You go back to your friend's house & wait in the call center queue. They get round to you eventually, tell you to immediately quit school.

In the double context of a sharp decline in the vocations and of an interrogation as to their identity connected with the aggiornamento of the Congregation, the sisters of Ribeauvillé in their majority left teaching, not by force as in Congo-Brazzaville, but through retirement. Though some of them, in the scope of the institution, chose to undertake new activities and to live within pluralist communities.
— Luc Perrin

The Desert Catapault

The shadow of Giorgio de
Chirico arrives outside
the railway station even
though it isn't one. Else-

when, clouds exit from
the tunnel, & a wooden
mannequin has a pepper
shaker shot into their eye.

He Is Not Speaking

How do we interpret
this? That the woman
controls the man &,
no matter who is act-
ually speaking, it
is the woman's voice
that predominates? Or is
it an acknowledgement
that people are fluid
beings, polyhedronic, &
that sometimes hiding
behind the mask that
faces the street is one or
several of the genders
we are made up of?

The Prince of Objects

Static or dynamic — the ontology
of most games depends upon

a division between the objects
in play. If one is lucky, the dynamic

can occasionally be seen through
gaps in the static, not that we always

recognize what we see. The dance
is different in every decade. So, too,

the music. Once there was tea for
two. All died when u went away.

The Female Thief

is a conundrum that is sometimes found in jars of honey.

finds that creativity, rather than spirituality, is more efficacious at
keeping loneliness away.

recently completed the translation into Farsi of many exemplar
sentences that all contain the words "recently completed. "

has been given the green light to explore & develop gas on 164 sq km of
land with high potential.

has accumulated five annual depreciation charges, reducing the book
value of her lock-picking tools.

is beholden to the glass ceiling for damping down any public opinion
that a female could be a highly competent criminal.

used the Rugby World Cup to break down barriers to the gospel in
sports-mad Japan in a way that has left local pastors amazed.

continues to break down barriers by showing how ethical clothing can
hold its own on high-end catwalks.

relaxes by playing along on drums to tracks by Charles Mingus or
Thelonious Monk or any other dead jazz musician who can't complain
when she occasionally loses the beat.

sometimes wishes she were male, like Fantômas, so that — despite her
reservations about exposure — she could be well-known enough for
René Magritte to want to paint her.

Une simple histoire d'amour

All she left him when the
relationship ended was a

chair. Decorated with a lion's
tale to remind him how

boastfully he had entered. Of
such small size that it was only

the humiliation of dismissal
that meant it fit him at the end.

from *Aube à l'antipode*

> On the other side of the
> globe an hourglass over-
> turns. There is no
> breakage. Even so, things start
> shutting down. Dusk arrives.
> Here, the stage is empty
> until Lionel Ritchie appears.
> He breaks into song. Sings
> *All night long*. In the un-
> seen audience we see a man's
> face fracture as if it were
> a mirror. Dawn breaks.

La Bonne Fortune

& in the supermarket I
buy a pack of pickled
pigs' ears for the alligator.
He doesn't eat them —
dietary or religion I'm
not sure which — but it
carries a simple message.
Stay in line or watch out!

& for the pig I buy a faux
alligator-hide handbag.
She's a lovely animal, &
will appreciate the gift;
but, once again, the mess-
age is aimed at the 'gator.
Step out of line, & the
next one won't be fake!

I go to lunch; the sniping
starts again behind me.
Pig in a poke, I hear from
the pool. *Gator so full of*
sugar it sold out for that
added aid comes grunting
from the pen. I can't be
bothered quietening them.

Still Life

The tensions ensure that life
is never still. A cathedral or

a school, angular, unplugged,
slides off into the grays &

blues of night. A man moves
forward. He is wearing a mask.

Eyes move along the side of
his head. Birds sing on the

sidelines, not that there are any
of either there. Bards sing in

the background. Keeping them
quiet & still is always a problem.

The Invisible Mirror

The white caps of the waves
are replicated by the shreds
of clouds floating above the
water. The lower clouds are
solid like the continents
above. Angles of reflection
& refraction insinuate the
painter is lying on his back
to complete the composition;
but if that were so there is no
sign of him. At least, not vis-
ible. He has obviously moved.
This is a record of his journey.

L'esprit comique

Unable to see out, & sick
of being adorned with
flowers or vines or those
ugly plaques made from
clay that have the faces of
Roman gods embossed
upon them, the trellis has
decided to escape. Donned

disguise & cut it to shape.
Certainly ends up making
it a figure of fun; but it's
fine to breathe through, &
light enough to stride easily
over miles of countryside.

Foolhardy

The dance floor is con-
fined by mountains of
ice. The ice is also on the
dance floor but is not
for dancing on, though
some have tried. Have
failed. So badly that
they need to call upon

another of their other
selves who also have
come crashing down. A
lesson learnt. Not even
the fanciest mustache can
improve one's balance.

A line from René Magritte

It's a bleak view of hu-
manity. Facing eco-
logical collapse, Freddo,
plus a whole host of

Cadbury characters, went
beyond science to shine
a spotlight on transgender
issues, using their jittery

art-punk guitar buzz to
offer a frayed life-line to
the most vulnerable people.
The snowoman wonders

what the world offers them
outside of that. An ability
to handle subzero temper-
atures? They have that already.

The Dead Bird

for Hannah Weiner

No matter how
many times she

opens & closes the
wardrobe door,

the bird behind it
remains dead, part

in, part out of
its ungilded cage.

Sugar Bowl with Fruit & Books (1923)

This could quite easily be the
table of a diabetic, given that
when you Google the individual
components, that's what most of
the responses seem to suggest.

Then change the order, books
in front, & the preservation of
the species leads the way. Not
the human species, not at first.
Push past the jam & conserves

& you come to why sugar is bad
for you, can lead to an early death —
but reading some expensive book
might help you put that off. An-
other permutation, with the bowl

back in, & ceramics from Amazon
loom large. Probably what Magritte
had in mind all along. Who belongs
in the sugar bowl? Why steal Céz-
anne's apples? Where is de Chirico?

Man in a Bowler Hat

Is not a prototype. That came
some years before. The title
suggests it may not be a self-
portrait though of course it is,

even though this time around
we can't rely on the eyes to
confirm it since they can't be
seen — a dove covers a larger

area than an apple. It's the tie
that gives it away, as always
slipped slightly below that
apex of the collar where the

shirt is buttoned. Only the tie's
color changes. The man does
not. The bowler hat follows
what current fashion dictates.

The Music Lesson

Too late for a taxi, so the
teacher calls in a bell to
take her pupil to her home
out in the countryside.

They've done this before, is
well-rehearsed & dressed
for. The student needs only
to assume a slightly higher

register to become an ear, in
part a kind of signifier, but
also allowing her to hear which
way to go & give directions to

where the best seats are. The
bell keeps time. The ear be-
comes a part of it. The sinking
sun promotes the score, enabling

a different color to be heard.
Now the invisible is rendered
visible. This lesson is complete.
What will she learn next week?

The Lovers II (2)

The temperature drops rapidly.
Wind increases the supply of

oxygen. It was the cornice that
I noticed first, crossing wall &

ceiling at a point possibly re-
lated to the golden mean. Only

later did I realize their heads
were swaddled in white cloth.

Magritte on the Stamboul Train

A procession down the
street. Some dust, but not
enough to hide the images
that the horse-drawn drays
would reflect in the shop
windows should they have
had glass in them. Instead
wooden louvers, in which

the procession draws closer
as it draws away. A trick
of the eye says Magritte. No
more, no less. I paint what
I see, though admit others
may not see the same as me.

L'Automate

What is the *grelot* thinking
of now that it has finally
come to rest? Has assumed
the position, as it were, the
one that says traveling is
over for the day. Poses

for the painter on a velvet
cushion, inside a wicker chair —
not quite renaissance splendor
but close enough to it, given
the times. Is it thinking &/or
surveying the visible world

in front of it? Is it reflecting
the invisible one? Is this a
programmed move, a simple
act of recuperation? Or has its
power source drained, & the
binary pathways all dried up?

The Vulture's Park

A powerpoint presentation of
images related to the royal
Christmas visit to Penshurst
takes great liberty with the
meanings usually associated
with emojis. My communications
degree has lost all relevance, so
have parked it away in a small
box from where it talks to me
all night of the pain it feels
when a leaf falls. Outside,
Mother has turned the Palace
grounds into a croquet green
& now I'm waiting for some-
one to hit a ball though that
final hoop & knock down the
bonsai which takes the place
of the central peg. Maybe then
I'll be able to get some sleep.

The Rights of Man

You have the right to remain stationary & not promenade along
the promenade that runs along the edge of the sea.

You have the right to rest against the meteorite that lives there.

You have the right to allow your euphonium to catch on fire
&
you have the rights to any poems that might be found in the ashes.

You have the right to believe your euphonium could possibly
be a phoenix & thus rise up entire from the ashes.

You have the right to be embarrassed by your pattern baldness
& to carry an olive leaf to disguise it should anyone come along &
wish to talk to you.

You have the right to a cast iron street lamp provided it doesn't
have a bulb that works in it.

You have the right to a cloak to wrap around your shoulders
as protection against the storm that may be blowing in over the sea.

You have the right to a single glass of water. Sip it wisely.

You have the right to an attorney should you be arrested for loitering
with intent. If you can't afford one, one will be provided for you.

You have the right to personalize the name of that warning
by changing Miranda to Magritte.

La reconnaissance infinie

He stands on a globe
of sheet music to draw
closer to those lips. The
globe plays up like a
pianola, starts tinkling

beneath his feet as they
stir it to life. The song
that emerges is repetitive—
rock my heart it goes, over
& over. Then the lips open

& invite an even closer
approach. It's a siren song;
but he recognizes that too
late as he is swallowed up
in to the dried-blood sky.

Elseneur

The trees grown up
& shaped to repli-
cate the castle that

once stood here. The
place no longer a
hamlet. Now over-

grown. No longer
a place for Ham-
let to call Home.

La Belle Promenade

Never one
of my strong
suits, eloquence. Think
of a fence. Either bricks
or blocks, laid
square, or wooden
palings, up & down.
Nailed. Cemented.
Everything in its
pre-planned place. Not
like that for me. I look
for stones, with shapes
that match & inter-
act when placed
contiguous or even
at a distance from.
Something to run
your hand across & feel
irregularities, perhaps
seen smooth at distance
but up close catch
the breath, cut the
fingers with their rough-
hewn balance. Strong
enough to bind,
to keep the dogs
from running
on the road.

Architecture au clair de lune

Some place in — is it? —
North Africa or southern
Italy, where, in the physical
absence of Giorgio de Chirico —
though his influence is every-
where — the moon is over-
seeing a game of *pétanque.*

A great play is made, but
only the stairs rise up to
applaud. No one else is here
to see it: the mannequins
& bilboquets have all gone
off to bed. Where they toss
& turn, the moon too bright.

The Idol

Position is everything.
That's why this stone
bird can only fly above
a stony landscape. Place
it over water & it would
fall & sink. Is shown in an-
other painting that it's birds
made from the air which
have all the advantages.

The Quandary of Painting

You have blank walls. I have
four baby turtles with painted
backs that arrived at Dulles
International Airport earlier
this month. So, let's start with
room use. As in: "What do you want
to use the space for?" &: "What
do you want it to say about you?"

La victoire (1)

The topiary of doorways
renders them ambiguous.

A surfeit of entrances. Few
ways out. Enter, & risk

entrapment. Otherwise?
Follow the line. It may end

in sunlight or continue on
until night captures it. There is

a difference between mazes
& labyrinths. A pattern

to one, the other full of
doors that are not closed

until you try to open them.
A passage is the space

between two doors. The space
is hope. The doors despair.

The Fountain of Youth

Last seen in
the Pyrenees.

Perched on a
peak. Small in

context but
omnipotent.

Now wraps its
wings around

a reed. Petrified.
Monumental.

The Key to Dreams (1935)

.....& then
there are
those rare
times when
our dreams
speak to us
in a language
we can under-
stand.....

La Trahison des images

En anglais cette
fois, but it
still won't give
you lip cancer.

Perpetual Motion (1)

So far the circus
strongman has
eaten a tiger (&
now wears its
skin), Alice, Albert
Einstein, & Annie
Edson Taylor, the first
person to go over
Niagara Falls in a
barrel—the evidence
is all around. He
feels no shame, is
still able to hold
his head up high.

Le Retour de Flamme

> His immense shadow spreads out
> Over Paris and the world.....
> **Robert Desnos**: *La Complainte de Fantômas*

The world asleep &
dreaming out loud.

Emanations cohere;
fear personified. In-

stead of rain falling
sur les toits de Paris

it is the shadow of
Fantômas. Dressed

for his own on-going
opera, as large as the

life he lives in others'
dreams. They would

have him with a knife
in hand, but this is his

reality so he carries a
flower. It is a rose. They

would have him dead
but it is their dreams

that keep him alive. He
does not dream of them.

A THEATRICAL EVENT. Juve has been on the trail of Fantômas for quite some time. He crawls along the broken cobblestones of a mysterious passage. To guide himself he gropes along the walls with his fingers. Suddenly, a whiff of hot air hits him in the face. He comes nearer...His eyes adjust to the darkness. Juve distinguishes a door with loose boards a few feet in front of him. He undoes his overcoat in order to wrap it around his left arm, and gets his revolver ready. As soon as he has cleared the door, Juve realizes that his precautions were unnecessary: Fantômas is close by, sleeping deeply. In a matter of seconds Juve has tied up the sleeper. Fantômas continues to dream — of his disguises, perhaps, as usual. Juve, in the highest of spirits, pronounces some regrettable words. They cause the prisoner to start. He wakes up, and once awake, Fantômas is no longer Juve's captive. Juve has failed again. One means remains for him to achieve his end: Juve will have to get into one of Fantômas's dreams — he will try to take part as one of its characters. —**René Magritte**.

The Spring Tide

The pre-
diction of
tides on an
a priori basis
is not possible.
Local conditions
apply. One works
from charts & tables—
how far the fall between
high & low, the positioning
of rocks, the shape of the sky.
What the weather is doing. Are
the Moon & Sun colinear with the
Earth? Do clouds collide with bells?

The Poet Recompensed

Implied self-
praise, inflated
self-worth. Used
dragon imagery
in his poetry — the
dragon guardian
of gold, & gold,
believed the poet,
was suitable
recompense
for all his work. For-
got the bit about
fire-breath & flame.
The dragon didn't.

La Plaine de l'air

Cellulose
per se
has a slow
metabolic
rate of
decay
so that
a leaf
separated
from the
tree will
still hold
its form, &
a fallen leaf
still vert or
held vert-
ically in
an unseen
web or by
the earth
creates a
tree in
space.

Le mariage de minuit

All questions have
been abolished
since no-one
is certain of the
answers anymore. The
Oscar winner weds
her boyfriend under
a candy-striped
tent somewhere
in the tames of
Alaska. He has
left parts of him-
self—his wig, his
face—on the table
back at the New
Mexico ranch. She
is annoyed, tears
out trees & plunges
the branches into
the earth where the
roots used to be. No
blindness like snow
blindness. He says
"I do." Still five &
a half months to
go before Spring
rolls around. You
may kiss the bride.

Les muscles célestes

The cavity in the
skull over-
flows with
the training routines
of Italian body-
builders. But where
is its zenith in
relation to the observer?

Titanic Days

Torn from Picasso, &
further torn—bather
from sea, or mother

from baby. The clothes
torn from her. Then
ravaged. About to be.

Victim & aggressor. A
classic dialectic. Shadow
given substance, form

taken on. Is classical.
Modern. Zeus in a
business suit? No

less likely than white
bull, white swan, a
shower of gold. He

falls across her, he falls
upon her. One outline.
The form taken on is

taken from Goya, Kronos
devouring one of his
children. Titanic days.

The Use of Speech

"A nondescript
form can often
replace the
image of an
object." &. "Some-
times the name
of an object
can replace an
image." Linnaeus
double-coded.
A personal
taxonomy.

The Betrayal of Images (2)

for Michel Foucault

> There is this
> treacherous space
> between the image
> & the text that
> many have misread &
> fallen into. I stand
> well back, let others
> with more sure footing
> describe it to me.

The Famous Man

Inset in velvet in-
side a box, the
bilboquet morphs. Chess
pieces, skittles perhaps. The
tower is de Chirico. The fourth
wall of the theater is partially
open. The back wall
is night. All around
an Escher frame.
A wounded bison
has been painted on the
wall just around a slight
curve in the cave. Long
ago. Cannot be seen.
Water drips, has dripped
through the roof ever
since, maybe before
the bison, after it
was seen, was
captured. A city
has grown up. The
man is stalactite. Per-
haps bat. Either way
is famous. Not as
famous as the bison.

The False Mirror (2)

Given a list
of words. Asked
to repeat them
back. A test
for veridical
memory. Eye,
reflection, looking-
& cheval-glass,
sky. Alice. All
synonyms of. Or.
Associated with.
Not included. Her
initial answer. The
thought made
visible. Mirror.

The Happy Donor

Aporia. The man
a product of a past
which was. Never
his. Constructed
from: metaphors
in a language no-
one speaks. Not:
any more. De-
constructed to
display symbols.
Not symbolic of
anything. Are
reference, points
to earlier paintings.
First used. Were
simple objects.
Given here. All
together. Symbolize
the painter. Not the
man. A bell. Out-
side the man. Is
real. Is the product
of a past. Was real.
Outside the man
the man is real. The
bell rings silently
to announce the dis-
mantling of its own
rhetoric. Aporia.

Les Promenades d'Euclide

The first events in the nursery are metamorphosis & settlement. Vertical fluxes vary over various timescales but retain the essential features of prediction equations—satisfying the conservation of mass & total energy. Any method that alters the data, whether by swapping, random noise or erasure decoding, is rejected by the differential circuitry. A monosyllabic type must produce harmony if the enclitic is unelided. As yet, there are no significant rock/non-rock preferences.

It's all fairly standard practice, but it's no surprise that a lot of money & brainpower are going toward customizing supply chain solutions. Restrooms are open to the public & are wheelchair accessible— motorcycle seats can be very uncomfortable. The saving grace of the nuclear family in history was the extended family that surrounded it.

By the time that David Bowie took his final bow from the whole touring scene at London's Hammersmith Odeon in July 1973, efforts to bridge the gap between phenomenology & the principles derived from perturbative & nonperturbative quantum chromodynamics (QCD) were an essential part of American pop culture.

New Year's Day this year fell on the Day of the Rat. The structure of the Euclidean algorithm defines a family of rhythms which encompass over forty timelines from traditional world music. The force between quarks does not diminish as they are separated.

Clear Ideas

Returning to the Moon is the key to humanity's long-term future in space.

It is a vertical project, akin to climbing a ladder. Each step has its own name, its own symbol. The symbols are not visual representations of the naming words. Nor are the names descriptive of the activity of the step. There are no milestones, only spaces between the steps.

Memory retains them thus, & can produce them to the mind whenever it has occasion to consider them.

The first step is called "A control toolbox automatically loading for no reason." The sea is its avatar.

The Ready-Made Bouquet

Ever the
bourgeois, never
daring to be seen
out wearing Botticelli's
naked Venus. Leave
her at home on her
halfshell, with the
clip-on ties. Wear
the clothed one. &
even then embarrassed.
Worn behind. So that.
One or the other. Her,
or his face. Never
both together.

The Discovery of Fire (2)

In the evening, before the sun set, she would write down those things that had caught her interest during the day. At one time or another she had noticed that she could tell how long she'd been away from home, how long before she had to head back, by the length of the shadows & the direction in which they pointed; how when seen through the smoke from bushfires the sun had a form to it. She noted the way animals tracked & trapped, or how they hid from one another, beneath surfaces or assuming the color of them. She worked out the cycles of plants, & was no longer surprised by the way fish would reappear from beneath the surface of dry lagoons when they started filling with rain.

Today, as the heavy rain clouds moved down from the north — direction was a concept she was still formulating, but she knew where the sun rose & where it set, & she also knew that, at different times, if she stood facing the sunrise, the hot wetness would come from that side of her face, & the even hotter dryness would approach from the other — she saw a bolt of lightning strike a tree, setting the oil inside it alight. She recalled a smaller spark she had once seen, when a flint axe brandished in anger had struck a cliff of a particular rock rather than the head at which it was aimed. She extrapolated; & realised that if she could find something combustible to trap the spark in she would no longer have to wait to find fire in the wild, would be spared the task of nurturing it, keeping it alive, something that took her away from the composite act of gathering food, information, insight. By forcing two objects into contact with one another she could produce something greater than them both, usually invisible, but there in the air, waiting to be called forth.

In this way Promethea discovered, first, poetry, & then fire.

The Search for Truth

      is
difficult
      if you're a
fish

&

      out
of
      water

      & you
don't
realize
      that

what
      you're
      looking
for

      is
what
you've
      found.

The Mathematical Mind

There is no
mantissa — all parts
are present &
counted for. But
the present is the
sum of parts of
the past; the
past is memory.
Sometimes there
is transposition
in transcription.

Memory (1948)

```
SOUVENIR
SOUVENI
SOUVEN
SOUVE R
SOUV ER
SOU  IER
SO   LIER
S   BLIER
    UBLIER
  OUBLIER
```

Souvenir de voyage I

Light travels
between
cultures &
continents at
its own speed,
remembering
where it's been
through multi-
tudinous
museums to
keep mementoes
in & a
sophisticated
mnemonic
technique
for learning
long lists. The
old also move
at their own
pace, but
keep it
simple, visit
few places,
retain few
keepsakes. They
are petrified
of travel, their
travel mementoes
petrified.
Little light.

L'assassin menacé

Il est si calme or
whatever the
colloquial French is
for staying cool
under pressure. Though
strangely inappropriate;
for the cool criminals
of the time were
not assassins but
mainly jewel thieves, a
long line of, mostly
fictional, Fantômas &
Raffles through to (if
not, should be) Sean
Connery. This is
more the following
fin de siècle, maybe
that's what he's
waiting for, the iPod
to replace His Master's
Horn & Hannibal
to get down off
his elephant &
take his place
on center stage.

Memory (1945) (2)

All I
can re-
call is a
bas-relief
head

between
a near-
full glass
of water
& an

apple.
The
apple had
blood
on it.

Les Pas perdus

Maybe aerobic exercise
is just as effective as
medication in treating
stress; but the idea of
punishing the material
form by sweating it out
in the gym is not my
idea of fun, doesn't even
move me to a basic level
of arousal. I'd rather go
to a traditional Chinese
medicine establishment
where they give full-
body massage or take
a trip to the discothèque
where there are no
wasted steps, where the
cognitive components
of dancing counterpoint
the theme of survival &
may in some way relate
to everyday functioning.

L'Homme au journal

"I'll fill in those
other panels
after I've been
to the Club &

seen if there's
anything in
today's paper
that inspires me."

The Invisible World

Sound travels
across the silence. Some-
where sea but this
is train noise. Or.
Trucks on the road
a mile or two
away. Cannot be
seen or. Cannot
be heard. In-
audible. Or.
Invisible. There are
other worlds
out there hanging
in the air, come
down to earth.

The Scars of Memory

Every time there's
even the slightest
scent of censure in
the wind, winter
emigrates. Reincarnates
itself as a wandering
Mariachi carrying only
an icy cold pitcher of
vermillion in its guitar
case. In stark contrast
the rest of us go
stereotypically retro
& relive the 1920s,
not sure how we got
there or why we've
ended up channeling
Shakespeare in some
hell-drenched backporch
reliquary of the mind.

The Interpretation of Dreams

1—

When larvae are reared
on acacia, almost all
larvae live to be-
come adults. Egg
size does not affect
larval survivorship.

2—

The "greatest toy
since the Game-
boy" is either
perfectly designed
for ankle breaking
or useless because
players find they
still can't jump
over tall buildings.

3—

We are sorry but
due to licensing
restrictions by
the game publisher
we can no longer
offer this game.

4—

The wheels on the
bus may go round
& round, but the wheel
from a bike is just
fine for holding
three framed screens

playing, on a continuous
loop, time-lapse images
of ceilings burning.

5—

2.5 g potassium nitrate
2.5 g ammonium chloride
33 mL distilled water
40 mL ethanol
10 g camphor

§

My seahorses group together at the base
of their tank holding on to the wire
frames we give them to sleep on. Explanations
sometimes include effects of electricity
or quantum tunneling across the glass.

6—

Only by appreciating the terrain, enemy, & friendly forces can the
commander identify & choose those times & locations at which
favorable conditions can be achieved. Fundamental combat skills
remain essential for battlefield success. Our Doctrine is Basically Sound.

The Present (1)

Most birds fly. Aero-
planes are almost
able to, achieve flight
only by manoeuvring
in the air as they
start to fall
out of it.

La Page Blanche

Echoing
both science &
religion, Magritte
suggests there
can be no
such thing as
a blank page
since the
invisible is
everywhere
just waiting
to be made
visible.

Reconnaisance without End

for Márton Koppány & Nico Vassilakis

One should conceal
the fact that one
is an adept, said Mr.
Behoover to his
Hungarian friend, &
that it takes an
endless supply of
lifetimes learning
how to become one.
Don't advertise. Adopt
a slightly eccentric but
innocuous code of dress —
1920s bourgeois with
its coats & sticks &
bowler hats is good —
then join a self-focused
group like Cloud Gazers
Anonymous where every-
one's heads are lost in
them & no-one notices
if you forget your-
self & start to levitate.

La Lumière des coïncidences

Optical efficiency.
The angles. The
candle is illuminated
by the woman's
torso. In
turn, re-
sponse. Refraction.
Light bounces
back. Angles
again. & curves
of shadows. A
scientific fact,
no coincidence.

Threatening Weather (2)

Mainstream American theology —
a.k.a. "the spinach capital of the
world" —informs this picture of
Yosemite Fall; but the efforts
of humanity to liberate imagination
are found more in dance &
ritual than in the sadly artless
subtitles of theology. In the
tea room of the sky we sip
non sequiturs & sup on slices
of graffiti peeled from real
railroad cars. The weather
threatens. It's what we came for.

The Literal Meaning II

salon hair
gods false
trap death
bell door
rail guard
balance trial
idea bright
time prime
spectrum broad
room drawing
avant post
black token
drama high
fire forest

The Literal meaning VI

It is the
body of
a woman,
drawn &
quartered.

The Golden Legend

Lapis philos-
ophorum — the
philosopher's
stone. &. Loaves
& fishes. Miracles?
Legend? Every-
one is entitled
to their own
beliefs about
the stuff of life.

The Castle in the Pyrenees

Each summer would
move to the house
up in the mountains. Sit

outside at night, de-
code the stars. Plan
journeys by them,

direction, distance. De-
scribe the places; fact,
fantasy. By day

would trace the travel,
to see what of what
we dreamed was real.

The Flowers of the Abyss I

Hélas! tout est abîme
wrote Baudelaire—*all is*
abyss, a completely
automated world of self-
assembling machine-flowers
made possible by an
emergent form of video
expression. Each change
brings out new curves in
the shoreline; in the same
ambient space there is a
region where the perception
of the image is still affected
by the dead blue screen. A
message appears to say
there is a problem with
the file. *All windows*
bare the infinite to me.

The Flowers of the Abyss II

A curious eclipse—
traffic regulations now
require night to have
a bell that absorbs
light without refraction
fitted to it. Times past,
an event happened, we
rushed out & ran to it
in rampant schaden-
freude. But this is no
accident, is mechanistic;
so we stay within the
ice-blue interior of a bare
carcass of concrete &
play chase the dog or
describe Nigeria or clean
graffiti off the wreaths &
potpourri. Shorn of its
exits the sun is quiet.
Time stands still, bells
hang heavy in the air.

The Annunciation

Squeeze the symbolism
for all it's worth. Olive
trees in an otherwise
barren & rocky land-
scape, the simulated
organ, the confessional
latticework. No real
people, not even foot-
prints. Wooden bilboquets
have turned into pawns
& vainly wait for someone
to move them. It's a
sterile oasis in a forty-
day desert, which
someone once found, an-
nounced its discovery, &
was famous ever after.

Le Portrait

Dans les plus sombres yeux
se ferment les plus clairs

were the lines by Eluard
that caught Magritte's eye.

La Plaine de l'air

Even though the air
is an unstable
medium at best, the
tree, a plain text
ASCII file made of
everyday materials &
the common language
of commercial signage,
stands unmoved. Else-
where, the German
Army is entering Paris.

The Ladder of Fire

He had noted the
nesting order—how
the paper fit in-
side the bell of the
tuba & it, in turn,
rested on the chair—
so that, once this fire
was over, they could
be neatly stored until
the next time he
had need of them.

The Adulation of Space (1)

Try to unfold complex
polyhedra & the
kinetic barriers
create a problem—the
configuration of power
no longer holds when
automata are abstracted
by collapsing their
states. There is between
the universal &
particular a reciprocal
tension that cannot be
confined within an
allocated space. It's a core
drawback of pattern re-
cognition, made more
so in the figurative
when flesh holds sway.

The Meaning of Night

The man walks
away from him-
self, the woman
hides in her hair.

They ignore each
other. Wherever
they are, neither
is dressed for it.

All around there
are fallen clouds.
There is no moon,
faint light, the man

casts a shadow. The
woman cannot
see it. It is night
inside her hair.

La Ruse symétrique

At 4.30 he
brought
the clothes in
off the

line. A
nightdress
was missing;
so, too, his

mother. Weeks
later they
were found,
water-logged

& with a
symmetry
she never
had in life.

Les Six éléments

As of this
writing, there

are 137 Magritte
items available

on eBay. They are
mundanely pre-

sented — none of
the six elements

that Aristotle con-
sidered essential

for drama are
in the frame.

L'Amour désarmé

The key-
words —

Clothing, Military, People, Religion, Transportation, Headwear, Army, Adults, Groups, Naked People, Woman, Women, Christianity, Religious, Land, Hats, Soldiers, Christian, Cart, Wearing, Clothes, Armed Forces, Transport, Head Wear, Adult, Group, Naked, Nude, Female, Lady, Females, Ladies, troops, Combatants, Kneeling, Tying, Weapons, Outdoor, Helmets, Armour, Swords, Square, Kneel, Kneels, Outside, Outdoors, Exterior, Exteriors, Open air, Openair, Armor, Weapon, Sword, Triumph of Chastity, Love, Disarmed, Bound, edifying, historical legendary, Petrucci palace, Penelope, Suitors, Rome, Signorelli, Trionfi, Triumphs, god of love, bound by Laura, ideal, chaste, Petrarch's poetry, Lucretia, chaste heroines of antiquity, heroes, Romans, Caesar, Scipio Africanus, exhibits, prisoner, triumphal car, victory, tied, path, arrest, caught, chasing, wings, virtue

— are else-
where.

L'Île au trésor

> Birds
> in / the trees
> are / the trees;
> leaves &
> trunk.

If I repeat this definition I'm no more than a parrot. One must come up with an equivalent. — René Magritte

> Trees
> in / the birds
> are / the birds;
> feathers &
> wings.

Puisqu'on ne peut changer la direction du vent, il faut apprendre à orienter les voiles. — James Dean

> Trees
> are, birds
> are:
> feathers &
> trunk.

I don't like treasure voyages on any account, & I don't like them, above all, when they are secret & when the secret has been told to the parrot. — Robert Louis Stevenson

> The icon-
> ography
> changes. The
> Germans
> are in Paris.

The Promised Land (1)

I don't know what the
19th century saw in
the letter *S*. Perhaps
its classic look re-
minded them of the
sex & violence that
were once associated
with pressed metal
ceilings. These days
even the private space
of public figures
is made from wood.

The Night Watch

i. The endocrinology

I stroll out to Wilshire Boulevard.
A group of part-time soldiers are setting out on parade.
There are bits missing.
A lot of raw fish has a tendency to do that.
"I'm a NASCAR fan," she said at a
birthday party in little osaka one recent night.

ii. The interval between first & second sleep

Marie-Ange sounded determined.
It was reflected in
her elegant handcuffs.

iii. Prolactin, a pituitary hormone

There's no longer a difference between theater & shadow —

"I saw Brazil last night, Terry Gillem. Never saw it before.
It was boring. I had to watch Chronicles of Riddick to clear
my head of thagt junk."

Today I get to prep for a colonoscopy.

iv. Unlike meditation

Montanna's
just a
pathetic
wannabe troll
with no sense.

v. Altered consciousness

He prepared a candle-lit gourmet dinner
that would end up being eaten
by the mangy dog on the front lawn.

vi. Benign states

The babysitter got bored & went to watch TV.

La Tempête

She is everywhere but
       here, the naked woman
   who / dresses like a bank
       clerk, infatuated by the
   costumes of the era of
the play. Elsewhere the
       art is concert, is full
   of irrepressible gypsies
       who blaze with hothouse
passion, & men who swim
       for twenty hours in
   sideways rain & seas
       as tall as magnesium.

An End To Contemplation

paradoxical sleep
a recurring sleep state during which dreaming occurs
in which the person is aware that he or
she is dreaming while the dream is in progress
lucid dreams

short rib ravioli ($16) arrives on a puddle of "natural broth"
meteorite hits Peruvian village
only a fence separates Point Roberts from a bustling, strip-malled
suburb & a
short commute to a hip, urban downtown

a luminous object that produced a loud sound
shaped like a cell that is about to divide
pure utopianism
filmic dissonance
essentially tests of the null hypothesis

a Foucault test uses interference patterns produced by a knife edge
to determine the deviation of a mirror from its ideal shape
Foucault the first to show how a pendulum can track Earth's rotation
mechanisms acting during human sleep

the calligram immediately decomposes & disappears
leaving as a trace only its own absence (the other Foucault)
virtual apotheosis
the sign and intensity of the acting
may be a difficult goal to realise
solutions beyond machine learning may be necessary

sisters & their lovers in verdant present-day Hanoi
a traditional city with an increasingly hip, urbane edge
the comparative effect of factual & ideological propaganda
Stalinist aesthetics suspended
at half the focal distance

cells divide
the world did not come to an end
we may be too attached to protecting our image

The Universe Unmasked

Featureless cubes
   with facile inter-
weaving are the
true building blocks
   of the universe.
Carbon is outdated.

The Listening Room (1958)

Climate change &
predictions of future
climates have never had
any particular significance
for me. Theories are not
statements about the
world. To that end I have
done numerous interviews
for radio, television & the
print media as a prophet
who ascertains through
divination that the apple
we experience is just a
bundle of sensations in
synchronism; there is no
way that we can affirm
there really is an apple.

The Son of Man (2)

Non-event-
ually an
autobiopic

was made of
his life. It
was anony-

mous. Only
the apple
had a name.

La Magie Noire

Usually the second
name is abstract, the
name of a Madonna.

A naked woman leans
on a rock. Evolving,
gradually merging into

the blue sky. Sometimes a
bird sits on her shoulder.
Conjuration & invocations

are the basis of her formal
syntax. Earthbound, yet other-
worldly. Hanukkah gelt.

Not Esperanza but some
bird-name is revealed in the
first chapter. More Americans

believe in a literal hell &
the devil than in Darwin's
theory of evolution. The

second section describes
some practices children
engage in. Black magic.

L'Usage de la parole

No fence
    high enough
to shut out
the world. Some
    seepage. Con-
struct, concept, the
    allocation of
words, even
when taken
    out of con-
tent.

Le Panorama

A ball in the
air, no, a
bell. A horse's
bell. There is
a name for
them but not
the name that's
given here. This
is not a bell.

Les Amants III

Is the love
still physical

if, when the
face masks

are removed,
the body

floats
        away?

The Secret Life IV

Everything known
is in the room
beyond. This side
of the wall the
peacocks dance.

Finding the way
be-
tween is only
/ part of the
journey. The

rest is
recognizing
landmarks that are
/ not familiar. For
the well-versed

traveler
spheres are
a remedy for the
seasickness that
floats beside

them.

On the Threshold of Freedom

It was then that we
arrived, too late
to influence, but not
too late to interfere.

Le Beau Monde

The world which
we see
clearly

is the curtain
in front
of

the
world which
Magritte clearly sees.

The Companions of Fear (2)

The
Companions
of Fear are
to be

found
at the
top of a
mountain.

Fear is
some-
where
below.

The Flood

Only
her euphonium
kept   her   afloat.

L'Ami intime

All I
could offer him
was
     water &
bread. But we
are good
friends, & I
forgive him
for walking out
on me.

The Palace of Curtains III (2)

The curtains
drawn. Same

thing on both.
Sky. The sky.

Neither is.

The Search for the Absolute

Images &
things you can't
look in-
to. Gödel
again. The
absolute is so
uncertain. But
I have just killed
a small flying
thing that
landed on this
reproduction
in my Magritte
book & it is
now absolute-
ly dead.

The Call of the Peaks

Glaciers flow
out of the

painting. The
mountain is
an eagle that

does not leave
the ground.

Le Voix du sang

Gödel once
more. If a
forest is cut down
so that only
a single tree
remains, is
the forest still
part of the set
of forests? Let's
ask the people
living inside
the tree &
see what they
have to say.
There's a light on.

Threatening Weather (1)

Not enough to hear
the words. Had to see
how the mouth
curved around
them, how far the
tongue came forward,
how heavily the teeth
bit down. Only then
could he under-
stand their intent.

Le Philtre

I took my troubles
down to Mme
Gorgon. Zola
wrote about her, said
you can't even
smile & say
'cheese' be-
cause if you
look at her she'll
turn you into
stone. Then
take away your
bottle of *Le
Philtre Numero Neuf.*

Ceci est un morceau de fromage

The
problem
with
truth is
that it's
often
falsely
painted &
hard to
swallow.

The Kiss

The marble
was far too
heavy for
this land-
scape. Was
taken away,
but the
encapsulated
concept left
behind.

The Hesitation Waltz

It might be
embarrassing
not even having
two left feet
to get around
the dancefloor
on, but the
apples have
mastered

the complex
pauses of
the hesitation
waltz so well
they now
are forced to
enter dance
competitions
in disguise.

Memory (1942) (2)

She
     stepped
          down
from her
       pedestal
& ran off
to join
a circus. Not
what she
remembered
  from her youth.
  Centuries
of standing
  still
meant
she was perfect
as the
     knife-
thrower's
assistant. Never
scratched.
But outside
the show her
  refleshed
perfection
      made her
target for
the freaks
  who filled
out side-
show alley &
they drew
  blood.

The Palace of Curtains, III

I
see the
sky reflected in

this single word
you've left
me.

Enterprises of subversion & destruction

The polished surface throws
back the arrow. Beneath it,
handwritten in a painstaking
artificial script, a script from
the convent, is "an American

may possibly know the customs
of your country better than you
do." Visible form is excavated.
Shape dissipates. About this
ambiguity I am ambiguous.

To reproduce & to articulate; to
imitate & to signify; to look &
to read. What misleads us is the
inevitable futility of converting
the text to some glaring color

when a simple swipe of a rag
could soon erase it & reduce
phoneticism to mere gray noise or
inconspicuous article. Treasure
the pearls of what you have read.

Sources:
This Is Not a Pipe, by Michel Foucault
The Ladies' Book of Etiquette (1860), by Florence Hartley

The Art of Conversation II

Of late
my dreams
have been so
heavy
     I
find them
hard
to talk
about.

Le Musée d'un Nuit

It is
an over-
night stop, a
motel of
memory,
where some
of the guests
have the
provenance
to dis-
play them-
selves &
others
stay hidden
& wait
for room
service.

L'Eternité

Everything that looked
on turned
away,
even
small birds
whose eyes acquired

only outline, not
the detail.
Fear
frays
the hem-
line of eternity.

Who
comes to
save us now?

Les Fleurs du Mal

Je suis belle, ô mortels! comme un rêve de pierre
Charles Baudelaire: *La Beauté*

Sometime
I must check up on
why the statues
of antiquity
had no pupils. Would
have been easy
enough to do, a
drop of paint or
use the chisel as
an apple-corer. In-
stead left blind.
Deliberate. No need
to see who calls. In-
duce the dream of
flesh beyond the
stone through
flower wide open
& eyes wide shut.

La Belle Idée

I start to tidy up
the tapestry. The unicorns
worry me. Not the one
all gleaming white &
shiny-horned, it's the
other, the one with
the shades & lycra bike
shorts who's lurking –
can unicorns lurk? – who's
hanging out then, there
by the castle gate,
waiting for some corn maiden
to come tripping out
on her way to the
fields where he will follow
& (impale her)^2. Only
just then the Lord
of the Castle comes
riding up with his entourage
who all have earpieces that
drift down into their
chainmail & steely eyes
that scan the crowd, a-
lighting on the unicorn
who pretends he's looking
at postcards in a market stall
before sliding back off
into the background &
back to his nighttime job
in a porn theatre where
the prurient masses pay
to watch some corny maiden
get impaled by a quadruped
with a condom/inium on his head.

Memory of a Journey III

I know we sidetracked
to see where the
troglodytes had
lived. Other than that
think bridges gone
over, under, or
danced upon. & lines —
train, coke, telephone.
Somewhere we had
antipasto, & drank. Not
too much, just enough
to make conversation
easy & company
complicated. Towards
the end the waiter
brought a bowl of
fruit. We peeled the
oranges & fed the seg-
ments to each other.
We left the apples.

The Interpretation of Dreams

1) The Acacia

The arid regions
of Senegal
act as an incubator
for the
gum arabic tree.

2) The Moon

A soft
moon shuffle
by the light
of the
silvery shoe.

3) The Snow

The bowl of
night is
black
& filled
with white.

4) The Ceiling

ceiling
wax
lyrical

5) The Storm

The sky
has that angular
clarity that
often precedes
a change in
the weather.

6) The Desert

Only when the
last nail
is put in place
does it be-
come apparent
that all along
it was a
mirage that he
was building.

This is not an apple

It is the
most realistic
of his apples.
Slight blem-
ishes, variants
of color. Leaves
& scissor-cut
stalk. It is
what the painter
says it isn't.

Discourse on Method (1)

Having
suffered
through 17
symposia
convened
by L'Académie
Française
on *Le Discours
de la Méthode*

& fearing
he was
about to be
pushed be-
yond the
bounds of
rational
thought

Descartes
discarded
his wig
& his silk
breeches
& hose
& headed
for the
nearest
leather bar
muttering

"Who gives
a fuck what
anybody
thinks. I am
what I am."

God is no Saint

Either. It is
an absolute.

Or. It is
an absolution.

The bird
is perplexed
by the shoe
size &
is unable
to decide.

Le Trait d'union

The male   There it
  flower   encounters
   breaks off   the female.
    & rises
     to the   Birds
      surface of   grow.
       the water.

             The use
of hyphens with adverbs is redundant
unless an identical adjective exists.

Late-blooming sun.

The Search for the Absolute (1940)

Held
the leaf
up to the

light.
Said. In
this one leaf

the
entire tree.
Said. Is fractal.

Is
blueprint. Is
the entire forest.

The Lovers II (1)

Is said. Aug-
mented by
is seen. Sur-
text. Not under
but laid upon. The
emphasizing
hand, the under-
scoring smile. What
is read into by
what goes on
around. So
are the lovers
so aware of
one another
that inflexion is
nuance? Or is
there something else
behind the cliched
blindness?

La Joconde (1)

da
Vinc   i
would   be
pleased   that
Magritte   has
managed   to
capture   the
enigma   tic
smile   so
well   .

The Alphabet of Revelations

Only in so far
as asemic
comes first

is the
alphabet of
revelations

arranged
alphabetically.

The Two Mysteries (1)

Ceci n'est pas
une pipe. N'est
pas ceci aussi. Only
the painting is /
what it claims
to be. Is a
painting. Is
a painting of
a pipe. Or in
this case also
a painting of
a painting of
a pipe.

The Black Flag

The memories react
to basalt, the machines
remain the models
they once were.

Collective Invention

She has legs &
feet. So. Instead of
lying there deprived
of breath it might
seem reasonable
to think she would
try to stand &
see if that allowed
an easier flow of
air into her gills.
Except. Pushing
herself upright is
probably impossible
when she only has
fins to do it with.

Philosophy in the Bedroom I

The usually con-
cealed placed
outside. Flesh
on fabric, as if
the clothing were
internal. & we
have nowhere else
to look except
away. Which means
at some point
we have already
looked inside
ourselves. Were
frightened off by
what we found there.

Philosophy in the Bedroom II

Some times
we keep
our fetishes
in the closet.

Sometimes
we wear
them out.

Madame Récamier de David (1)

In this fromage to
Jacques Louis David
Magritte has
copied his portrait
of Madame Récamier
in intricate detail
right down to
the shy smile & the
burnished bronze
of the coffin handles.

Letters stand in utter defiance to spelling-book rules

The lost chatter of men, the
exteriority of written &
figurative elements—very
few persons write a good
letter. In this split & drifting

space, strange bonds are knit.
Two garrulous mutes use
elegant language, yet use it
easily. A word can take the
place of an object if the paren-

thesis is avoided. Neatness is
important. The measure of
the "iron horse" is how many
missives it drags behind. No
mass, no name, form without

volume. Word & object are
deployed in two different
dimensions. Emptiness undoes
the space. Verbal lightning
flashes come naturally to a child.

Sources:
This Is Not a Pipe, by Michel Foucault
The Ladies' Book of Etiquette (1860), by Florence Hartley

The Rape

kiss
my
pudenda

The Betrayal of Images (1)

Gödel said
that the
concept of a set
that contained
all sets
was impossible
because it
could not
contain itself.

Magritte said
that no
matter how
realistically
an object
was depicted
it could never
be
anything more
than an image
of itself.

In-
complete.
Agreement.

Ceci n'est pas une Magritte

Truckee.
210 kilotons.
Christmas Island, 1962.

Time Transfixed

It is the image that is
important
so
first paint
the painting
& then decide
what
the locomotive emerging
from the fireplace
might mean.

The Hunters at the Edge of Night

Usually he evaded the hunters
with little trouble. Only when
the dogs joined in
did he feel trepidation. They
spoke a different language. It seemed
more familiar to him
though at first he understood it
less. Finally he stopped running,
covered himself in mud &
became invisible. He learnt
the hierarchy of the dogs, the
patterns & cycles of their
behaviour. He killed the alpha male
just after the dominant female
came on heat then caught & coupled
with her. Now they hunt the hunters.

The Reckless Sleeper

At last! I'm glad to see
you've finally caught up
with the program. I've been
dropping hints for years
but for all the good that did
I might as well have been
pissing in the wind. Nothing
like smothering you with
a surfeit of symbolism. Over-
kill perhaps. But even that
mightn't have worked had I not
given you that book on Freud
for your birthday. Bet
the first thing you did was
try to find out what sort
of sick bastard I was to
pull a stunt like that. I'd
watch you reading it &
caught by something look across
at me. Back to the book then
back to me again. & later
I sensed you pausing in the doorway
as I slept, indelicately picking
the desktop icons of my dreams
like newly opened flowers
or fresh field mushrooms. Tasting
them, smelling them. So tell me
what you really think of me
now that you know me better.

The Magician

Do you believe in magic
asked John Sebastian in that
old Loving Spoonful song. & J.S.
Bach worked his own magic
when he
transformed mathematical relationships

into music of powerful emotion.
But transubstantiation
as myth or mystery
is derided by Magritte in this
act of prestidigitation
where the magician is the magic

& the actions commonplace. A self-
portrait of the artist having lunch,
fork in one hand, knife in another. The
third pauses with a piece of bread
before the mouth. The fourth
is pouring wine. No blood. No body.

Plain fare indeed for a follower of Kali.

The Bather Between Light & Darkness

The outside
inside. Light as
window/painting. Out
of context
would be a simpering
watercolour. Descending
strata of sky, sea, sand
arranged in a
possible logarithmic spiral.
Fibonacci sequenced. The
golden mean
in a golden frame.

Is bather only by reference to an earlier painting. She is nude. Is nowhere
near the sea though she lies stretched out on a carpet which could be
sand. Her face is angular, her head propped up by an arm bent to echo
the shape of the dark ball in front of her. Eyes closed but she is not asleep.
No-one can sleep in that position. Maybe she is imagining the sea, that
she is one with it. Venus without the halfshell. Curve of the breast, curve
of the belly, curve of the line from hip to knee — all follow the curvature
of the imploded star. Her legs aligned with the lines of light. So, too, the
line where the carpet meets the wall. She is in between light & darkness.
Possesses elements of both. Is possessed by neither.

Night as a black ball. Is
dark matter. In a posed-
card of the thirties
would be
held in front of breasts &
cunt in beachball modesty.
Only one breast is hidden here.

The Large Family

Giorgio
de Chirico
re-
invented
himself by
faking
his own
paintings.
Couldn't you
have borrowed
that off him
along with
those earlier
enigmatic
images
instead of
ripping off Renoir
or turning out
those works
that you
called
vache? Jesus,
René,what
were you
thinking
of? Thank
Christ you
finally came
to your senses
& returned
to the
real world
of men in
bowler hats &
birds re-
inventing
the sky.

The Empty Mask

If we give
objects
different names to those
they were made or
born with

are we changing
reality
or merely re-
arranging it?

If I
tell someone
that a chair
is no longer a chair
but now
a tuning fork

how can I
make them
agree with me

when they
already say
the sky
is sea & see
a forest as
the human body?

Laughter &
curtains
are interchangeable.

They is me.

The Seducer

The ship
the sea
is sailing on.

Birds
are made from
the air.

The house
we live in
is a
forest.

I awake
in my dreams
to find
I am only
awake in them.

Homage to Mack Sennett

Transparency in all
things or concealing to
reveal. We see
what we imagine. By
placing a sheet
of glass in front of
a naked body
we cover &
uncover. A curtain
would conceal; but with the
under image overlaid upon it
it is revealing. Put
layer upon layer
then peel them away. The
placing is the stuff of
slapstick. Displacing is
pure eroticism. Décolletage.

Perspicacity

Start at the
end or
end at the start. Axolotls
made sense
only when salamanders
were discovered. Over
easy or overtime
inspiration
is still just
a spark in the air. In-
vent the axle
& the wheel
becomes a double-
decker bus, dragons
once were eggs. In
retrospect
it is easy to see
how life cycles.

cicerōn'ē : a guide who understands and explains antiquities.

There is a
long list
of crops — maize &
manioc, tomatoes,
sweet potatoes
& a type of
lettuce — but corn the
most important
of them all. Ground
into flour, fed to the
animals, fermented
for beer. Half of
what was left
we kept for trade,
half to the priests
at summer solstice. Corn
was the keystone
of our lives.

Yes, we knew
about arches
& architecture. Some
had the skills
but still allowed
the priests to
tell them how
to build their houses.

& we
knew about
cornerstones
though to use
that term here
means we would be
playing one word
off against another
in a way that would
not please the gods.
We have been told
that humor that
is invented
is profane.

Roof & floor
the priests
to us, walls
& windows.

But houses
sometimes
need to
be rebuilt.

                    up to
    Once   the village
    a week   the   through
    we also   spiraled
    brought   temple.   that
    them   path
    animals   on the
    or meat,   position
    each   by their
    family   determined
                in turn,

In back of
the temple the
priests' gardens. Sun-
flowers
in one, peyote
in the other. A path
to the heavens, a
passage to the
depths. Sacred
plots, secret texts.

Sometimes
in spring or
early summer we
would walk the paths
that led up to
the mountains, to pick
the flowers that
grew just below
the snow line. &
sometimes we
would walk the streams
that ran down off
the mountains, to pick
up the gold
caught in the pools
as the melt passed by.

One
tenth
left to us
to trade
with.

The priests
believe in
a reverse
tithe.

Every year,
on a day we knew
but waited for
the priests to tell us,
we would melt
the soft metal
& cast it
in the form
of the family
totem. Placed
on the wall
but occasionally
worn. If a boy
had been born
the previous year
a new line would
be started. If a
girl, then a space
in the father's line.

Corn never
bought slaves

but where does
the priests' gold

go? It is rarely
our torn-out hearts

we hear howling
from the temple

each month when
the moon is new.

To end
a solar eclipse
the priests take a
young boy who has
less than ten
gold tokens
on the wall
of his family home,
wash him with water
from their private spring
& clothe him
in unbleached linen
which is
woven from flax
harvested near the sea.

He is given peyote.
He is laid on the altar.
He stares at the sun with dull eyes.
He sees darkness
before the darkness is seen.

A sunflower is
placed to replace his face.

We are gathered, watching.

We know what is to happen.

We know what is to happen

then.

As the moon
starts its
slide onto the sun
a brazier is lit. As it
continues to drift

twelve torches
set in a circle
around the altar
are set alight. & as
the moon
passes fully
across the sun
hiding it
like an apple
poised before
a man's face
a priest wearing
the skin of an ocelot
which marks him
as coming from
the same family
slices the boy open
from throat to un-
descended testicles,
rips out his entrails
& casts them
into the brazier.

It is done quickly. The
heart is still beating.

It is done so
we hear the first spatter of fat

just before
a fingernail of light shows

the sun is being born again,
the boy is dead.

This boy
whose smile &
eyes of innocence
remained
even as the
priests
took him to
the temple
the day before.
Never to know
experience. & we
experienced &
not so innocent
watching
wondering
how it is
the priests
need no help
to predict
the start
of an eclipse
but seem to need
such ceremony
to make it end?

The mothers talk.
The fathers listen.

The fathers talk.
The mothers listen.

About a kilometer
from the village
in a small valley
with its own spring
there is a garden
of daisies, one
plant for each local
sacrifice. The priests
tolerate it. Perhaps
inside their
passion
there is still
some compassion.

In a bend
of the river
accessible only by
canoe there is
a garden of
sunflowers. The
priests do not
know it's there.

Three-quarters
of a moon before
the longest day
two of us
took most of the
left-over corn
& a small bag
of secreted gold
& paddled
four days downstream
to collect the swords &
daggers ordered
some moons before.

On the way home
we did not speak.

Were afraid to give
a voice to fear.

This year, instead of
gold & corn
we brought the priests
iron at the
summer solstice. Their
deaths were slow
& not com-
passionate. They are
buried on the
other side of
the river, two day's
march away from
us. Their ornaments
are with them. The
jungle is
looking after them.

The raised center
of the village
is made even higher
by the pile of
broken mud-brick
that is tumbled
there. A set of steps
leads nowhere. Dead
sunflowers in a
parched garden. The
sun alive. The ocelots
are returning. Eclipses
come & go. Some-
times we eat the
peyote buttons
that continue to
self-propagate. We
share the visionary
world & teach each
other. We have
learnt not to make
that journey on
certain days
for then we
sometimes meet
the priests. So far
we have seen no gods.

The
train to
Machu Picchu was

full
of strangers.
I sat alone.

The Acrobat's Exercises

The random actions
of the acrobats &
the precision
of the clowns
contrast to create
a tension
which the ringmaster increases
when he rides into it
on a white horse
cracking his whip
& surrounded by
elegant assistants.

Such momentum.
Yet the progress
of the circus parade
is still dictated
by the pace
of the elephants
& the amount of shit
they leave behind.

The Secret Player

for Jukka-Pekka Kervinen

Master Class in that
a group of us
are brought together
& once we've finished
demonstrating our skills
are then shown
how it should be
done. Jukka as ice-white
tennis pro, serving up aces
while we watch on
amazed at the ease
with which he works the
court. Ice-blue, ice
as prism through which re-
flects/refracts all
colors, through which
neutrino words pass
to form ice crystals
sharp as stone, light as
lattice. Secret player
in that I have slim
sense of him outside
his poems, in that
the game he plays is far
beyond that which
the rest of us call tennis.

The Magic Mirror (1)

Is this an
ontological defence? Use
abstract name for
final output
rather than focus
on what concrete instants
made it up. If it's
ended this way
then you probably didn't
see them on the way through
anyway. Therefore not real. So
turn away. Turn out
the light not
caring if the
darkness remaining
in the mirror in
the room just left
is resident or reflection; or
refr/action of what else
was written there.

The Listening Room

An apple
on the table
is no threat; but
walk into a room
to find it
filled by a
giant apple.....

*

Had gone
to write "the apple
peers out the
window." Wrote
"pears" instead. A
slight tectonic drift
of associated words
done accidently &
unconsciously.

*

Magritte's
placement of objects is
deliberate, is earth-
quake territory. The
displacement of space
by things that should
not be there
but are seemingly
quite at home.

*

Maldoror in whom I dream apples.

*

Only a painter
could place
this giant object
in a space where
the entry
place & space
is so small.

*

Cliffs, chasms. A
precipice pre-
cipitated by the
unexpected. It is why
even in the light
we fear closed doors
& rooms that
may not be empty.

*

How large the tree?
Who picked the apple?

*

There are no
eyes. How then to
tell in
what direction
it is facing. The
apple appears
to be looking
out the window. Small
wordplay. All
the room
that's left to
manouevre
in. There
are no ears.

*

What is it
listening for?

On Apples

Once made
the comment that
Magritte would have been
better off if
he'd done
a de Chirico
& reinvented himself by
replicating his own
paintings. He
must have
been listening.

In 1952

& 1953

& 1958.

Only the landscape
is changed

(only
the landscape
never
changes.

Golconda

An image such as this
might have been
what the Poynter Sisters
had in mind when they
sang *It's raining men,
Hallelujah.* Or maybe
it was that other song
of theirs called — was it? —
Creole Lady Marmalade
with its refrain of
*voulez-vous coucher avec
moi, ce soir?* & they
were working on the principle
that if you ask enough people
sooner or later some body's
bound to come across
even if it is only
an anonymous Mr. Average
in a mass-produced bowler hat.

In Praise of Dialectics

He tried to
take over the discussion
by stating that the
principles of dialectical materialism
gave life to what might
otherwise have been un-
realized revolutions in
several former
European colonies. It was
a successful coup
but no-one stayed around
to acknowledge it. They
left through the window
& entered the house inside.

The Son of Man (1)

Does this apple obey
the laws of gravity
& fall at thirty-two feet
per second per second?

Does time move slower
in the reality of an unreal
landscape? Do objects
invent their own velocity?

Will the man take off
his bowler hat in time
to catch it? Will the hat
withstand the impact?

Why assume the apple is
dropping? Why not movement
in another direction. What if
it's the man who is moving?

What makes us think there is
activity? Couldn't this
moment of apparent intersection
really be an eternity of stasis?

If we know the questions then
why concern ourselves with
answers? & if we know the answers
why be concerned at all?

Isn't the painting reality enough?

The Flavor of Tears

I am a plant
with new growth
said the bird

I am
the underside of
the caterpillar who feeds
on me

I eat myself
It is exquisite agony

I taste my tears
as the caterpillar
eats them

Their memory
is etched
in my green flesh

Intermission

Peace
is popularly
supposed to be

the
period between
two wars. Let's

hope
then that
the actions of

those
who invaded
Iraq or blew

up
Atocha Station
were parts of

the
final act
of a tragedy

&
not part
of the intermission.

Cloning Magritte

The only hope I have
of acquiring some of
that European culture
I so admire is to ex-

hume Magritte & re-
move some epithelial
cells & grow them up
in an agarose broth in

a petri dish in much
the same manner
that Magritte did with
Giorgio de Chirico.

Attempting the Impossible

Trains weren't
invented
when they built a
railway between Bradford
& London. Leonardo
was designing airports
before he thought
about flight. The
model arrived
only after
Magritte
had painted her.

The Liberator

I have always thought
of the subject as
Italian. The patriarch of
a transported family, sugar
cane growers in North
Queensland, the first here,
able to speak a little
English, his wife far less
because she never mixed
outside the community. He
is a picture on the wall
or a watcher at the festival
parade, no breath left
to play the tuba in the
marching band, no longer
able to keep in step
with a step he never really
was in step with. Eyes
on an embellished past as a
diminishing present passes by.

*

I see echoes of my father
also. Non-Italian. Freemason.
The attache case with the regalia
hidden inside, the pearled
candelabra reminding me
of jewels & embroidered
aprons. He never talked to me
about it. I never asked. He
never talked because I didn't
ask. I never asked because
he never talked about it. Round
& round. We never came close.

*

Never a liberator. Quite
the reverse. A tight hold
on the family. Rationed
freedom. We escaped by
becoming birds or keys or
pipes or wineglasses. Every-
day objects that could always
be replaced. He never
noticed. The space inside
the outline is as it has always
been, a shadow of himself, how
he'd always seen us. The
eyes in the pearled lorgnette
are mother's eyes. She is
held tightly. A second cane.

The Pleasure Principle

A corona of light
like an un-
glassed light bulb.

Unsighted.

Seeing what
the sitter sees.

Alighting
at this
precise
moment
of space
this precis
of time.

Taken &
being taken.
The sitter
unseeing.

Unseen.

A moment
of insight
as we
who are
un-
seated

are taken

into a
space of time
we cannot
see.

Excited
&

anticipating pain.

Eternal evidence

The curve
of the jaw-
line is
the motif
that follows

the slightly
misaligned
body
down
past
the breasts

past the eye
of the navel
& thatch-
work triangle
of the crotch

to where
kneebone &
tibia top are
parallel
patterns
above
the final
amputation.

The feet
stand alone.

Homesickness

If these were
disparate objects
then their
juxtaposition might be
provocative

but here they share
a commonality, each is
equally out of place,
as in place as
the other.

If the lion
had the man's wings

then this might
be allegory,
the lion a gryphon,
a mystical creature
as he who is now
Mister Commonplace
gazes out off the bridge
as people have done
ever since the
first tree

fell across
a stream. That
is the thing
about bridges,
wings or
no wings.

The lion
without a cage, the man
within one. Reality
is always

somewhere else. Only

the bridge exists,
hiding inside
the yellow fog
of melancholy.

The Lost Jockey

The photosynthesis machines
are down. Chlorophyll
is in short supply. Each tree
left only with the exposed
neural pathways of a
single leaf; but cauterized
by cold these are excised
from all external stimuli. Un-
able to smell the snow
or touch each other or
taste the passage of
this horse & frantic rider. The
forest is full of trees who
cannot see they're there.

The Secret Double

In Charleroi where
I grew up
the horses' halters
were hung
with round bells
like those that decorate
a jester's cap. When I
moved to Brussels
the same. A fortuitous
continuity. Later
in a Paris without the
presence of horses
I painted the bells
suspended above a
landscape that ran down
to the sea. I dreamt
of the afternoon windshifts
that would shake them
so I could see
their sound. Now
I have found you &
torn your face away
to show the bells embedded
in your memory. It is
a carillon we share.

The Empire of Lights (1967)

For the
nineteen years
between her husband's
& her own
death, Georgette Magritte
kept this painting
on an easel in
what had been
their shared house. How
hard it must have
been for her
knowing that after
their forty-five
years together
she could have
finished it off for him
with barely a break
in the brush strokes.

The Giantess

(after Baudelaire)

In those times when
Nature couldn't
get enough of it,
spitting out
on a daily basis
children who were
literally monsters, I
would have loved
to have lived
near a young giantess
even if it meant
the only way to
dampen my desires
was to insinuate myself
around her ankles,
a frotting cat at the
feet of a queen. That way
I could take part in
whatever perverse games
she played, could see
her body & soul thrive
on the freedom she
found in them, tell
if her heart hid some
dark flame, if that mist
that swam across her eyes
was tears or the
humid warmth of
pleasure. & as a cat
I could be leisurely
in my exploration
of her body. It was
magnificent. I'd
gently climb the slope
of her knees, taste
her thighs, tangle my claws

in the thicket of her
pubic hair. & sometimes
in summer, drained
by the sun, she would
stretch herself out
across the countryside
& I would risk the
crossing of her belly
to sleep below her breasts,
in their shadow, a
peaceful village at
the foot of a mountain.

Carte Blanche

"Visible things
can be in-
visible," said Magritte
about this painting. "If
somebody is
riding a horse through the
woods, at first you see
them & then you
don't. But you know
they're there. I
make use of painting
to render thoughts
visible." Then he
galloped off
leaving the rider
hiding the trees &
the trees hiding her.

Elective Affinities + The Key to Dreams (1927)

Put two or
more things side
by side or one
within another. For
the first it is
the space between
that makes the
magic, the juxtaposition
of things known
to create the unknown. &
yes, Isidore Ducasse, I
hear you laughing
in the background. It is
a collision that marks
the start of a new
journey. The in-position
is continuity, an egg
for a bird, or confusion
when something is
given an entirely different
name to that we
usually ascribe to it. Is the
briefcase labelled sky
to be our travelling
companion or the cover
under which we
set out on what
began a journey
& is now a vestibule?

Magritte's Deathday

She has
just discovered
that Magritte
died on the

very same day
she was put in-
to jail. What a
price to pay. If

she'd had
a get out of
jail free card
she could have

been going to
René's 106th
birthday party
later on this year.

Familiar Objects

Floating objects are a
common enough theme
in the paintings of
Magritte. Over-
done it could almost
be said; but not quite
since suspension
requires a suspension
of belief, & each painting
is refreshed & re-
freshing, creating
its own unique
atmospheric pressures,
a re-awakening
of surprise. Here
we have a singular
form seen from
multiple aspects; & in the air
the singularity
of multiple objects
that have no right
to be there, held
in suspense by
a single held-
in breath.

La Lunette d'approche

When asked
what color he
would use
to depict infinity
Magritte declined
to answer. "No
point in asking me"
he said. "Today
my birds are green,
yesterday they
were blue. I have
no idea what they'll
be tomorrow. Best
ask Georgette. She's
the one in the family
who has the better
distance vision. She'll be
posing, peering past
me; & suddenly
she'll say 'Instead of
a cabinet in the wall
behind why not a
window? It would
make the room
seem so much
larger, & I could
look out to the sea.'
& she's right, as
always, so of course
I do what she asks.
But only in a painting,
& with an infinite
blackness still behind."

The Therapist II (1962)

Adding the image
is a form of
cheating. It is
a way of letting
Magritte do
most of the
work. You give a
small misleading
glimpse, a kind of
precis without
the precision
of the original. Pre-
tend to read his
mind, inaccurately
fitting the painting
to your description
of it. Still the shill
from sideshow alley
though now you
work the avenue
in front of the
Gallery, promising
that inside will be
found creatures who
are half man, half
beast. & once the
money is collected
don't care that
small birds give
the game away.

The Age of Enlightenment

I took it to be
the effect of altitude
on particles of
light. Their
reaction to it.
The young were
not so sure. Spoke
of signs,
of revelations. Un-
able or unwilling
to accept
that even when
the air is thin
the aspects of a face
can have a
separate gravity.
The balloon
I offered up as
proof that hot air
rises. They understood
that. Enlightenment
is of an age. Is
not an Age of.

Memory (1945) (1)

The
introspection of
a severed head.

The Domain of Arnheim (1)

How can
a giant bird

lay
such

small eggs?

The Therapist (revisited)

for Nick Piombino

I know that
asking you to lie down
on the couch while I
sit across from you
is a bit old-fashioned
but humor me, it comes
from doing my studies
in Vienna. The bag
beside me contains a
peregrine falcon whose
purpose will become clear
later on. The wall behind?
A piece of *trompe l'oeil*
I asked this Belgian painter
to do for me. The sea is
so soothing. It's where
we all came from, it's
where we all desire
to return. Why? Think
amniotic fluid, think your
mother's lullabies. & the
birds inside the cage? At
first they're something
for your mind to focus on
while I explore the skies
they used to fly in. As we
progress, I gradually get
you to transfer to them
all the concerns that keep
you planted in the earth.
When that is done we set
them free. The final act
is to release the falcon.

The Companions of Fear (1)

Yes, I know my
shift finished
four hours ago
at midnight. & no,
I didn't get the
instructions wrong.
I've been doing
what you asked,
researching
the properties
of the chitinous
exoskeletons
of this group of
owls. Have done it
how you asked
me to. Started by
taking a small piece
of the carapace
and examining it
under the electron
microscope. You
were right. I found
fractals instead of
feathers. But I
didn't expect the
contradictions. That
the sample would
be warm & the re-
action of the birds
so cold. I thought
they would be
angry. It was
their silence that
frightened me.

The Song of Love

Perhaps a
piscine Rodin
this mer-
couple made
from the same basalt
as the shore. They
could be
singing. Is this
the song
of love? (& again
the ship the sea
is sailing on.)

A scene
that does not
seem to sing of
anything except
the Byzantine archi-
texture of
de Chirico's
mind. A stage-set
for a theater
of the absurd.
Pinned on a wall
a glove, a blank-
eyed bust. Green ball
in front, rooftop
in behind. & yet
this is the
siren song of
love that
fifty years before
made Yves Tanguy
jump from
a moving tram

that made
Magritte

say he saw
thought made visible
for the first
time. Making the
possible
improbable
but not
impossible. Pictures
within pictures.
Songs within
songs. Of
love. & other
strangeness.

The Central Story

The hand
at the throat
that holds
the veil in
place. The small
euphonium. A
closed suitcase.
Death &
departure.

As a
reference point
it would be
hard
to go past
the central story
that the face
of Magritte's
mother
was covered
by her
nightdress
when
her body
was taken out
of the River Sambre
after her
suicide.

Case
closed.

But what
would we find
if we
opened it?

The Lovers II

Memory does not
hold its
shape. Blurring
occurs. Always tricky
getting the light
right & how
much of the
initial energy signature
of love can be
retained? Things
change, return as
indifferent faces
in different
settings. What lasts
is how the lovers
shared a space, not
how they looked
at one another.

The Red Model

This
is a painting
I have
wanted
to write about
for some
time

but
the need to
leave my feet
at the door
for fear of
dirtying
the carpet

has
always
constrained
me.

Perspective II: Manet's Balcony

Whether it be
fête or
theater

or just

sitting
on the balcony
watching
the funeral
parade pass
by

Manet
insisted

his family
always dress
to reflect the
occasion.

The Art of Conversation I (1950)

No chance
assemblage. Too much
structure in the
way the blocks
are stacked. Look
at the base. REVE is
real & not
a dream. Foucault
describes it
as a landscape from
the battle of the giants
against the gods;
but if that
is so then
someone has come along
afterwards &
tidied up. Added an
after word. Re-
written history.

The Month of the Grape Harvest (1)

Open window.

Many men
in bowler hats.

The same man
over & over.

Looking in.
No looking out.

A sealed room.
Hermetic fusion.

September.

The Future of Statues

for Vincent Ponka

It was the
elegance of
the diving birds
that caught his
fancy. That,
& the fact the sea
was made
from stone. He
closed his eyes
& let the sky
stream over
him. The clouds
contained a
hint of snow.

Dangerous Liaisons

She held a
mirror up
to herself
then turned
away from it,
almost as if
this brief
liaison with
her own flesh
held too much
danger to be
confronted.

The Explanation (1)

Just as in
Edwardian
portraiture

it is the off-
spring who
is lying on

the ground.

The False Mirror (1)

sky
in the
eye

The Empire of Lights (1954)

Noisy birds silence
the trees. Someone
is reading as they
sleep. Against the blue
the house has braced
for night. Entrance is
gained through a door
in the roof. The pond
is full of stars. A street-
lamp echoes. The sky
is empty. Only clouds.

Pleasure

Blood stains
the white
lace collar.

How else to
test the reality
of flesh

than to bite
through feathers
& frail bones

& let the
blood dry
on your tongue?

Other birds
watch. Wait
their turn.

Some things
are not taught
in school.

The Threatened Assassin

No sense of inner
motion. It is
the eye that
activates, starting
with the mountain
outside the window
& spiraling counter-
clockwise round
the room. The assassin
seems unthreatened
by it all. The
naked woman lying
bloody-mouthed &
lifeless on the un-
clothed bed
is a past he is
indifferent to. No
different to
his appreciation of
the watchers at
the window, the net
& leg-armed
blunt force trauma
waiting by the door.
If time restarts they
may present a
possible future, but
in this one tableau
only the music
captures him.

The Legend of the Centuries II

The little chair
sits on
the enormous chair

even though
neither chair

is there
for sitting on.

Dwarfed by
la création
le créateur

or)

the Greeks
the Romans
will conquer.

Irène *or* Forbidden Literature

Levity & lemonade
for dinner. What changed
your mind? No matter.
I went along with your
desire to dance. Pushed
the stairway into a corner
of the room to give
us more of it. You
moved around me. I
kept time by ringing out
the rhythm on the bell
balanced above my finger.
Your first steps reiterated
your name. What else
they wrote there
I am not allowed to tell.

Memory (1942) (1)

Just as the
seasons & the sun
& the position of
the other
stars start
growth in plants
& birds to
fly to imprinted
destinations

so, too, do
anniversaries of
certain incidents
in the life
of Giorgio de Chirico
cause bells
to fall silent &
fall to earth.

Antiquities weep
blood. In the
Byzantine piazzas
of the labyrinth
pigeons pause
& whisper
Hebdomeros.

The Use of Speech

Words mean

only

what you think

they mean. Others

may see them

differently.

The curator takes his work to lunch
for René Magritte

Hungry midmorning
so ate
part of
a Cézanne
still life. The
varnish gave it
a toffee apple
feel. Decided on
a Braque fish
for lunch. Looked
around for a
suitable companion,
considered the
Renoirs but
decided they had
the potential
to eat too much.
Finally chose a
nude from Picasso's
Blue Period. Disappointing.
Her
asceticism was
appealing but there
was no depth
to her conversation.

Les Mémoires d'un saint

The theater
in
the round

is
open to the
sky.

The sins
offstage.

The House of Glass

Sonic
booms after
the sound barrier
is broken break
glass. The
speed of light
equates with
Einstein. Curved
space, looped
time, a Möbius
infinity of
simultaneous
starts & endings.

The Art of Conversation III

A bull
in a state
of grace,
although
alert enough
to seem
alive. Birds in
silhouette, al-
most a word,
the land
above, the
sea below. A
pace behind
unseen &
silent, she stands
parenthesized
by columns
listening to
everything
they have
to say.

The Happy Hand

The distances de-
fined. & by default
the spaces in
between. Balanced
relationships. Without
which the fingers
would not harmonize.
Some things taught,
something less
learnt. Practice makes.
Not perfect but im-
parts some form
to it. A semblance
of. In part. Way there.
Waiting for. What
is brought to it.
Outside the span.

Musings of a Solitary Walker

He does not think
about the water
he walks
beside. He walks
without it. Another
river. The Sambre.
His mother's
suicide by drowning,
her nightdress a
veil around her face —
but that's another
painting. This is
the Rue Morgue,
levitation, the corpse
laid bare. He does not
think about her. She
is a disquieting muse.
He leaves her behind
on the bridle-path, walks
on alone. Apples &
umbrellas will
eventually overtake him.

The Lost World

In the surrounding
countryside
trees define
the type of horse
that might be found
there. The contours
suggest a woman's
body; but with a
different angularity
some have seen
it as an empty
bowl of fruit. A figure
loses its memory
along with its outline.
Words wilt in the
winter heat. There
are no dinosaurs.

À la suite de l'eau, les nuages

After the water, the
clouds. After clouds
the telephone. Then
the hope that
someone will hear it
ring. After the answer
the question. Who
picked the flowers?

The Wedding Breakfast

The Christian fable
is loaves &
fishes. For M.
an egg. The lion
is an early piece of
microwave technology,
its presence agitating
sub-atomic particles
in the air. Two minutes
& the egg is boiled. The
wedding ceremony takes
a little longer. Priests
prefer convection ovens.

The Misanthropes

So great
their hatred
of humanity

they plant
heavy drapes
to keep it out.

A human act.

Magritte in North Queensland

There are no clouds. Let
me add some. A flock
of rainbow lorikeets
animates the sky. Let me
make them one bird
& take the color
out of it. Translucent
so the light shines through
but leaves some substance
in behind. The sky
darkens at the arrogance
of the act. The land
is consumed by the sea.
Imagination's orphan
becomes *La Grande Famille*.

The Human Condition (1933)

We
are one
with the landscape.

L'Arbre de la science

Leaves of
sword
& horse

& trunk of
curtain rod —

how does *your*
garden grow?

The Origins of Language

On a day sometime
before, & about which
the weather was
unknown, he climbed
almost to the top
of a pinnacle of rock
&, armed only with
a palette knife & a
sable brush, cut
away the apex
to leave a flat
platform. So that,
on the next
fine day, with only
a few clouds about,
he could climb to
the very top & dive
into the sea, thereby
giving the people some-
thing to talk about.

L'Esprit de Géométrie

Most
of us
would say
the faces
have
been ex-
changed

but to the
mathematical
mind it is
more a
trans-
position of
figures.

The Discovery of Fire (1)

Taken away from its
normal context of
fire & legend, the
phoenix cannot
stand the
scrutiny. The most
beautiful of birds
no longer
with us. Self-
propagation
can only last so
long, especially when
there's only one
at any given time.
The matter of the myth
degrades. Comes back
as something simpler. But
still suffused with fire.

The Apparition (1)

Windows on both sides leather armchair
card table foldup ping pong table. A colorful
oriental rug is seen. The colonel sat back
asking for news about the outer world. His hands
were concealed in the cloud of the horse's
lifted mane. It grew dark
in the weird silence, broken only by the
faint crack of a rifle. The white lines became
ghostlike; star-shells arched & finally melted
into the ambiguous cloud-land over the horizon.

(assisted by the late Leevi Lehto's Google Poem Generator)

Bel Canto

He would stand
before the mirror &
practice the gestures of
song. Outstretched arms,
the slightly oval O
of the mouth, chin
down on the chest
but not inhibiting the
flow of air. More
the reverse, draining
the diaphragm just
as his teacher had
shown him. Get
the technique down,
she said, & then I'll
show you the notes
that flow from it.

Magritte Tie for Alex Gildzen

Deep Waters

for Alfred Hitchcock & Tippi Hedren & Alex Gildzen

Unlike most
of Magritte's birds
is neither egg nor
simulacrum. With
blood. Wondering
which way to turn.
Le sang froid will
take the woman's
coat from off her
back. Or. *Le sang*
chaud will whisper
in her ear &
wake her from her
statuary. Or even *le*
sang trés chaud.
Will influence a
Hitchcock movie.

Magritte's Deep Waters   (p 205)

The bird
might be whispering
in the woman's (statue's)
ear.

It is a
neutral bird
wondering
which way
to turn. To
whisper in the
woman's ear
& make her
(member statuary)
or steal
the coat.

Nor is it
an egg.
The bird is
solid un-
like most other
Magritte birds

Unlike most the
Magritte birds, is
neither egg
nor phantom.

The moment
of decision

398

The Tomb of the Wrestlers

In what
was the
listening-
room

is a
rose

that has re-
placed
the
apple

is a
rose

& placed

is a
rose

a sleeper-
hold

on
this rude
stein-girt
domain.

La Lampe Philosophique

Ceci n'est pas
une pipe, c'est
un récipient
pour les narines.

The Married Priest

Over & over. Re-
peating the images.
Replaying them, the
same, a different
game. Con text,
context. *Trompe
l'oeil.* The outside in-
side. Men in
bowler hats, al-
one, all one, in
pairs, in conversation.
Horses' bells, birds.
Euphoniums on fire
or else deprived of
air. Georgette. That
which Ernst called
phallustrades, the
bilboquets. Leaves
that are the size of
trees. Lost jockeys.
Eggs. Fantômas. Un-
altered words with
altered meanings.
Clouds, & apples.
(Though sometimes,
fearful of being re-
cognized, the apples
might wear a mask.)

Hegel's Holiday

A glass to
keep the water
in, an umbrella
to keep it out.
Joined together.
Thesis / antithesis /
synthesis. Hegel
went off on
a holiday. All the
work done for him.

Elective Affinities

A civil
celebrant, Magritte,
a union-
maker, who brings
disparate things
together &
creates an arc
that leaps the
gap between
them. On
one hand.
On the other.
Relationships
exist, affinities
not always ob-
vious. & yet so
obvious. Such
as that which he has
elected to display
here. But sparks
still fly. So might
the egg if
re-
leased
from the cage.

The Hereafter

There is no inscription
on the tomb. Except
for the tomb there is
no inscription on the
landscape. What
will be written after
is already written here.

The Anger of the Gods

Most of the day they
paced themselves,
taking it in turns
to ride, to drive, to
sit behind. But as they
neared the top of
Mt. Olympus, the gods
grew angry at such
equality & pushed the car
a little faster. Nothing
seemed to change inside.
On the roof the rider
struggled to survive.

A found homophone

I go into Google
looking for a link
for that last poem.
Type in the title. Only
text references. I
re-enter, this time
in French, *La Colère*
des Dieux. The re-
sponse: "Did you mean
la couleur des deux?"
I misread *deux* as *yeux*.
No, I reply, I already
know what color
the eyes are. Octavio
Paz once gave me
a blue bouquet.

The Delights of Landscape

Even if the
store-room is full
the hunter still
goes out to kill
more animals, to
cut down trees &
so remove all
groundcover. Some
thing to trade with.
Or. Fresh meat for
dinner or for the
dogs; perhaps
the head hung
in the trophy room.
The wood is set
aside, seasoned
for furniture, or used
to fuel the fire
in winter. He has
made a frame from
the best timber. The
final trophy. To be
hung in celebration
the day the hunter
comes home with
his catch-bag full,
the landscape empty.

The Difficult Crossing

Hand holds the
frightened messenger. Even
the bilboquet looks
scared. Lightning; &
waves that reach
across the ship
to shake hands on
the other side. Walls wait
with spaces cut
to hold the windows.
Later the curtain
will come down.

The Threshold of the Forest

In the march
of civilization
there may
come a time
when the
artifical forest
is indistinguishable
from the
natural city.

The Man with the Newspaper (1)

for Hannah Weiner

> Each depends
> upon the other. The
> man with the news-
> paper, the room
> pretending
> he isn't there.

Portrait of Georgette Magritte

Sine
qua
non

La clef des champs

The key to the
fields was
a phrase employed
by several of
the Surrealists. A
less literal but more
precise translation
would be the door to
freedom, escaping
the asylum. On first
reflection that is what
this broken window
might depict. Except
the glass has
fallen inwards.

Personnage méditant sur la folie

Do we
reflect
on mad-
ness
     or
do we re-
flect in
sanity?

The Magic Mirror (2)

In-
voking
snow-

shoe
urinal
or

hand-
held
mirror

all of
which
antici-

pate
some
aspect

of the
human
body.

Le Seize Septembre

The
sixteenth
of september

was like
any other
day until

a tree
rose be-
hind the
moon

as
night
fell.

Observations

#1

There is half a moon in the sky this afternoon as I take the washing off the line. I think it has some-thing to do with the rampant inflation that coats the current world, how once you could afford a full moon, now the same amount of money only buys you half.

#2

I am reminded of that Magritte painting, *Le Seize Septembre*, as the moon makes its way upwards behind the large tree that stands between us. In the Magritte, it is a new moon rising in front of the tree; here the moon is almost full, & the tree has regained its normal place in front of it.

#3

There is a total eclipse about to begin. I am sitting on a chair on the back deck. Between me & the moon is not only that tree but, in the time it's taken for the moon to clear the topmost branches, around 3000 fruit bats have passed by, off on their nocturnal foraging.

#4

Dead birds punctuate the highway. The moon is nowhere to be seen.

Le Calligraphe

Winter is coming. We
have prepared for it.
Have written over &

over on any place we
could lay a brush on,
"winter is coming." We

have written, & now
the snow has fallen, &
overwritten everything.

La Maison

In what is essentially a
compromise, a sound system
      has been custom designed
        to enhance the teacher's
ability to communicate, to
reach out to students, to

      turn memorized inform-
ation into communication
        & expose the brain to a
rejigged language structure
      that makes the describing
        of strange structures easy.

La Belle Captive (1931)

The grape harvest is
over, so no window
full of staring men in
bowler hats. Just a
single man walking
along a grassy path,
not even significant
enough to be included
in the painting of
what might be behind
the painting if the
painting wasn't there.

Scheherazade

The Marquis de Sade —
also a favorite of the

painter — spent a literary
120 days in Sodom. That

was slightly more than a
tenth of the time it took

Scheherazade to convince
her husband to cancel her

execution, & at least a
1001 times less enjoyable.

The Window (1)

Not even pivoting on
one foot for an hour or
so in what passes as
the real world will give
any indication of how the
pyramids were built. For
that you have to bury
your head in the sand at
half hour intervals & at

every fifth burial vary
things a little & raise
your legs up into the air
in a kind of ostrich yoga.
Cheops will eventually
come along; & with him the
visitors from outer space
who actually oversaw all
the construction work. Levi-

tation, levers & pulleys, a
thin magnetic strip along
which monorails ran – talk
of them & the aliens will
laugh. What they did was
offer debt relief to various
third world economies in
return for their labor. So
the Inuit carved the blocks,

giant apes carried them up
the ever-increasing slope,
& Native Americans with a
head for heights & the benefit
of laser sights put them in
their anointed place. & all
the while bands played on
the nearby dunes with sub-

sidiary groups beamed in

from other Δ states in Central
& South America plus the U.S.
Federal Treasury, while aging
rock stars who pretended to
know something about eco-
nomics gave audiences to
the Pope & ex-Presidents &
-Prime Ministers in return for
knighthoods & naming rights.

Par une belle fin d'après-midi

Premonition or preparedness
or perhaps a personal per-
spective. Even at a young
age, even on holiday at a
château in the Alps, sitting
on the granite balcony during
a beautiful late afternoon, the
members of Manet's family in-
evitably impress by a readiness
to address Death & their dress
sense when they're doing so.

Le Pont d'Heraclite

Everything flows, no-
thing abides, eyesight
is a lying sense, wrote
Heraclitus long before
he'd seen the Magritte.

So, is this a painting of
an optical illusion, or an
example of the chemical
process known as sublim-
ation? A pipedream that

the bridge is incomplete,
or a solid transformed to
the vapor state without
ever passing through the
liquid? Doesn't seem to

worry Heraclitus either
way. Couples are things
whole & not whole, what
is drawn together & what is
drawn asunder, he posits.

Then, more in keeping with
the theme, he notes that
much water has passed
under the bridge & just hap-
pened to rub half of it away.

The Conqueror

Trees rise, dunes
fall. Nothing takes
the fancy of the

man in the tux &
fancy shirt. He's
board, is bored,

doesn't know the
first thing about
how to conquer it.

The Truth In Her Jasmine Bouquet

The dunce's hat comes from the tops of the towers where Euclid walked.

A kernel of wheat falls to the ground & dies.

Dreaming of pickles denotes vexation in love but final triumph.

One must have a huge amount of money to extinguish the fumes of the false Renaissance.

Hiring a private detective may be one way to go.

La Femme Cachée

In the last pages
of Breton's *Nadja*
he has moved on
from the eponymous
subject & is ad- & un-
dressing another, un-

named, woman who
has "taken his heart."
To him a replaceable
object. Idealized but
essentially unnoticed.
Hidden, in forest or not.

La Grande Famille

birds
are made
from the air

A Little of the Bandits' Soul

I applaud main-
stream dystopia —
that depiction of
personal & collective
suffering in modern
Chinese novels or a
new Japanese gothic
stenchcore band

with female voice.
Perspective is a funny
thing, a little iron cot
hanging to the side
of the stone wall in a
manner that's executed
with a little more soul
in its synthesizing.

The very latest in
wood & gas fire-
place options plays
titanic crust tunes
with some very
well placed cello.
When does Indie
stop being Indie?

Freedom of Mind

Big pipe. Low price.
No data caps. Leave
anytime. It's almost

a recap of a *Sons of
Anarchy* episode—the
new moon, a half-naked

woman, with some sort
of avatar, a pipe-dream,
clenched in her hand.

Pandora's Box

The rose waits beside the
man. Or. Maybe moves
beside him if the man is
walking across the bridge.
Twilight. The man is
wrong. The street lamps

are on. Or. Perhaps the city
is on fire & the lamps are
off. The rose is white. The
man is wrong. No matter
which brother. If Prometheus—
brought fire. Now waits to

see how his gift is taken. The
lamps are off. The man is
wrong. If the other brother—
Pandora's husband. Her
beauty given to him. A jar.
The lid ajar. The gift is

mothbite, fresh horror re-
leased, by a woman's hand.
But a second visit. The man
releases hope. & man-made
myth. Apple fallen far from
its original tree. History re-

written as his story. The man
is wrong. Is patriarchal, is
parody. Is intended to
disguise there was no evil
given by the original creator.
Gaia, the Giver of All Gifts.

Presence of Mind

Neither fish nor

fowl, am some-

where in between.

À La Rencontre Du Plaisir

Griot is troubadour,
  West African, live
    archive of traditions,
    much like the
      medieval minstrel.

Grelot is bell—jingle-,
  sleigh-. Usually
    small, unlike the one
    depicted here. Is
    a mystery why

the bowler-hatted
  man is focused on
    it since it has no
      mystery. The man's
      shadow stands be-

hind the curtain,
  looks in a different
    direction, absorbs
      the atmosphere. He
      will sing about it.

    Later.

The Uncertainty Principle

"An object (a human figure
or something else) is presented
against a background on which
its shadow falls, with the amend-
ment that the shadow is that of
some quite different object.
Example: a naked woman
projecting another in the form
of a bird onto a curtain."

Magritte

The title is totally abstract.
The painting presents a
disturbing aspect of
actuality. The uncertainty
principle means that the
position & momentum
of either subject or
reflection cannot
be simultaneously
measured with precision.

Early Morning

The door was open.

Everbody was lined up waiting for the door to open.

We had arrived early that Sunday morning, with
                friends from Wisconsin, so as to be
                among the first people to enter after
                the door was open.

The icing on the early-morning cake was little Georgette
                relaying to her mother that she enjoyed
                drinking a Starbucks with me as we
                waited to be let in once the door was opened.

Access was available only through the Modern Wing
                entrance.

The door was closed.

Celestial Muscles (2)

The most superficial, most
Yáng system, mimics

Kim Kardashian's facial
expression & stylish top-

knot, & comes from the
merger of ordinary bonnet

needles & Alexei Nemov's
fit gymnast body as he steps

out for the Prince's Trust
Awards in a stunning LBD.

Elementary cosmogony

It's the same
principle as
picking the wine
to go with your
meal, except in
reverse. That first
leaf you consider
often determines
what sort of day
it's going to
accompany.

Personal Values

an example of how technology helps citizens
what happens when the teacher mixes two colorless liquids
a prototype or a final version of the product
the ruins of a shipyard in the port of Carthage
a figure slightly hidden so that not everything is given away
the components of rapid installation
the yellow flowers of a sweet broom bush
a tongue removed from a cow with wooden tongue
the famous model of ancient Rome
two packs of insulation
a honey bee larva placed on a labeled glass slide
that timing is everything
victims of the Titanic stacked in body bags
an example of an optic nerve
Swedish glamor model Natacha Peyre posing with a fan
a mystery light in the distance
a cartload of seaweed
Earth as a small dot from a vantage point millions of miles away
the start of the dance with Death
only one moment & a cropped one at that.

The Famous Man (2)

He is floating upside
down; but still man-
ages to write about

air pollution monitoring
& source emissions
sampling. Is full of

concern for the dog
whom the maid is so
roughly ordered to

take care of. It is during
this time that any space-
craft traveling to Mars

must be launched.
Lessons do exist for us
from the Paleolithic.

Transatlantic Passenger

The horse has lost his bell
& balls. Not even half-assed,

just a tail. Has found a
muscular man whose nose

adopts a fencer's stance.
Cummerbund captured.

Wrapped. Bound. Might be
a fit. Tight, but enjoyable.

La Belle Captive (1948)

              She paused to let
          a brass band
                    pass—these days
          the beach was full
      of them. Not from
                any new-found universal
                      desire for music; rather
          a re-discovered   need for
          uniforms. Not winning is
                  never easy—especially
              when you also haven't
      lost. But the games
              are never over until
          the games begin. So
                    redefine the space
      between with passing-
                  out parades &
      swimwear & get the
          answers ready
                      for the questions that
      are sure   to come.

Night in Pisa

Close by the un-
edifying surface
images of under-
ground bombing
I come across the
Martha Graham
Company dancing
Stravinsky's *Le*
Sacre du Printemps
& stay with that.
This is not denial
but a necessary

maintenance
of balance.

Querelle des universaux

rock	paper
Wittgenstein	scissors

The Masterpiece or The Mysteries of the Horizon

Can there be) an infinite)   )
process : with a beginning

in the water — air comes
from water, earth from
water — always some :
     other kind.
        The boy does
not come) from the) man)

but from a learner / a man
of science is being made.

The former
        must have
an end. That
        which
exists after the
        coming to be.

The Connivance (1)

The design of modern
operating systems often
uses religious privilege
to conceal the results of
wanton destruction by

an unscrupulous timber
mafia. This rejection
of classical architecture
allows a 'natural' organic
building style to attract

rare maritime species to
locations whose décor
would otherwise suggest
nothing less than Dickens'
eponymous *Bleak House*.

Almayer's Folly

The low frequencies
of the spectra cause
horizontal rasta
distortion but
not all rock bassists
use it. There are no
step
      by
         step
instructions & the
assembly manual is
made with interfaced
flannel lining &
cotton fabric stretched
over the terrain be-
tween dilation & erosion.

The Witness

Shortly after
crossing the Earth's
meridians, the
paradigm shifted
to be replaced
by a single central
index letter. Hun-
dreds rioted. Sniper
teams lined the
walls. Pre-
booking for Good
Friday services
became essential.

The Literal Meaning V

She thought it was a fitting moment to remind us that doctors are working on developing a uterine transplant procedure featuring allegoric imagery, & with a surprise pop-up on the side. Some commentators believe it has much in common with the medicine stick of a shaman. Others scoff, say it's just another horse behind a curtain.

The Return

The temperament
of birds. Cardboard
container of take-
out noodles masquerades as
a nest of eggs. Light.
Elongated? No, not
that, the things it
touches. Ensuing.

Mesdemoiselles de l'Isle Adam

It can be hard
to stand out
        amongst one's
peers: so the
    necklines of
        the light blue
silk gowns are
    low & the rose-
    colored boots
    all have bro-
    cade tops. & to
top it off, who
    can forget a
band—or was that
    brand?—name like
    Telepathy-gabble
& Structured
        Exercise? Tell
    me again. Why
    do I need viagra?

The Fifth Season

A trial does not change
minds so much as
reinforce what people
always thought they
knew. It is for this reason
that we take a particular

interest in individual &
social learning. A while
ago the corpse was
quietly interred. I now
believe it is time to
re-examine his doctrine.

The Human Condition (1935)

Inside the
outside

    is much
    the same

as outside
the outside

    except
    there are

far fewer
people.

Saucisse casquée

                To disguise the popular
          Paganisms of the
            Day, the Africans
                  introduced okra,
              the Spanish spices
      & red peppers. From
      a wacky conference
  center situated in a
                flying saucer, the
          Food Standards
      Agency announced it was
                  considering taking
          legal action. Those Germans
              sure take their
          meat very seriously.

[Composition on a Sea Shore]

The long piece should be sized so that whoever is going
      Put your spices front & center
It never ceases to amaze me how incredibly misguided
      A shaman, showman, teacher & tireless debater
Naive animals were placed in the center of an elevated
      The first exhibition was of twenty-five trained
An inexpensive & simple accessory that enhances
      A very ordinary subject for a sculpture
The turnstile industry is one of those industries you never
      They had seen through the fog of the early
Will soon be made in the land of wooden shoes &
      Cross-contamination concern widens pet-food
When is something more than the sum of its parts?
      Shown here are homemade balls
Women's 2007 is in stock & available for purchase
      A Catholic Father of five lays bare his
They can now prove once & for all if vampires really

The Ordeal of Sleep

I like
painting
Georgette asleep
as much as I
like watching
her sleeping; but
it's an ordeal
for me unless I
take her night-
dress off &
paint her lying
on her side. I
cannot forget
how my mother
was found
after her suicide,
floating on her
back in the
river with her
nightdress up
over her face
as if it were
a veil.

The Orient

The source is probably *The*
Source, that, elsewhere
anadyomène, Ingres nude who

pauses, poses, water pouring
from a ewer resting on her
shoulder. Who has grown

bored with the stasis of it
all, put down the ewer, torn
it open, then climbed inside.

La Clairvoyance (1936)

First pose the
bird, & then

paint the egg
as it appears.

The Invention of Life

Very little is known
about the early life
of Archimedes before
he invented personal
flotation devices. It

could be him here, in
some sort of Chinese
movie, *middle-class
woman, hidden man,*
considering the placebo

effect, or the drift of
religions into new
forms, & wondering if
they change the way we
think about medicine?

Fine Realities

Isaac Newton
has been invited
to lunch. We are
all waiting for
the apple to fall.

The Chorus of the Sphinxes

fine quality home-style egg noodles, gourmet & organic pasta

approximately 80 actors & crew attended the party

we create cirCus that moves the heart, mind & soul

most likely represented the voiceless pharyngeal fricative

by continuing to browse the site yOu agree to our use of cookies

the fashion industry was in desperate need of some fresh air

at the core of oUr teaching, research, & public service

an inventor & visionary who did not limit himself to one field

the standards for registered providers set out the obligations

all poetry is copyrighted by the author

producing custom paneled & Sublimated sports apparel

underpinned by a truSted heritage spanning over 30 years

a preParation of human immunoglobulin for intravenous use

a creative studio which deals with design & illustration

we were able to bring three of the children

local & overseas musicians from diverse genres

the authoritative index of geocoded Australian addresses

a long drive through the Midwest

maximizing the potential, beauty & value of Space

461

La Clairvoyance (1962)

A common mistake people
make is assuming that 'seeing'

unfound objects or actions
removed in space or time

involves the use of the eyes
in a closed state. There will

undoubtedly be skeptics
who demand scientific proof—

repercussions from the
Human Genome Project—

but watch the video before read-
ing on. Due to copyright law

restrictions these images are
not available for your country.

Painted Object: Eye

When one eye moves,
        there is a ghostly after-
    image that follows it.

            The other eye contains
analytically defined
        shape equations that

    produce the ability to
            perceive color. It's
    always fun to dream.

The Cultivation of Ideas

He stands at the
end of a diving
board, the pool a
palette with limited
colors. Or so it

seems. & yet. The
man reflects upon
the pool. He has no
idea how deep it
is. Until the dive.

Table, Ocean, and Fruit

We are beyond frustrated.
He finally has real reviews
by real people. My hair has
become healthier. We live

in a house overlooking
the ocean. But we both
appear to have a texture
problem, either the toes of

clunky leather boots or/&
cuba libre & tropical fruit on
a wooden table. A player

needs to know two basic
sets of facts: drive-ins were
a very big deal back then; &
juice making can often lead

to exotic states. We're brand
new to power auras. Some-
times they just crash. What
is it we are doing wrong?

This is a Piece of Cheese

for Yoko Ono

This is a piece of the old Atomium, in the Delft University of
        Technology
This is a piece of information that is used to support a main idea
This is a piece of genre Koten from the Chikuho Ryû & Oshu Kei
        Schools
This is a piece of socio-political commentary
This is a piece of relationship advice.

This is a piece of paper I hand cut
This is a piece of some sort of map
This is a piece of code
This is a piece of metal folded over one edge of the disk
This is a piece of wood. Is this interesting?

This is a piece of three strand nylon rope
This is a piece of coral received from Captain Bob
This is a piece of thylacine cartilage
This is a piece of cloth that covers the face
This is a piece of another paragon's encasing amber.

This is a piece of a basalt pillow
This is a piece of cardboard so doesn't include a battery
This is a piece of cutwork lace that begs the question
This is a piece of machinery that simply isn't meant to be airborne
This is a piece of hardware that allows one item to take the place of
        several.

This is a piece of the Berlin Wall
This is a piece of metal in the eye
This is a piece of California's past
This is a piece of prime real estate
This is a piece of sky. Hold on to it.

This is a piece of art
This is the only piece of art we've left on the Moon
This is a piece of reality so dense that it goes beyond art
This is a piece of cheese
This is a piece of my puzzle now.

The Alarm Clock

      The alarm
clock tells me
        it is time
        to get up-
        side down.

Checkmate

Bored games. He
puts a pawn to his
head. The pistol

moves one space on
a black diagonal. What
checks depression?

The squares are empty
except for a sign in
one. Am I his avatar?

The Marches of Summer

Cubes float. There are
parts of several torsos
piled one upon another
so they do not float
away. It is daytime.
The light comes from
inside the room. The
sky is / not the sky. Do

the clouds pass through
the cubes or vice versa?
No depth. Some *trompe-*
l'œil. Much grammar but
overall ungrammatical . . .
& the war inevitable.

The Torturing of the Vestal Virgin

1. a-little-black-rain-cloud reblogged this from y0ungprinc3ss
2. m-u-t-e-d reblogged this from rumcum
3. **gentleheartslikeshotbirdsfallen reblogged this from madnessandwonder**
4. aeuum reblogged this from madnessandwonder
5. **madnessandwonder reblogged this from genitalya**
6. **genitalya reblogged this from knickelback**
7. rabidjoy likes this
8. **knickelback reblogged this from infestedmeat**
9. infantille likes this
10. kill-girls reblogged this from fouled
11. troublewillfind likes this
12. no-rmalities reblogged this from patholysis
13. poutypeach reblogged this from bludgen
14. amusementandlostcontrol reblogged this from magrittee
15. **trinityera reblogged this from fouled**
16. knickknack006 reblogged this from patholysis
17. zxcvsdfer4 likes this
18. necroparty likes this
19. **fouled reblogged this from thirdeyeblinded**
20. xdpollo reblogged this from in-terdicto
21. bateria-baja reblogged this from lentejon
22. lentejon reblogged this from addressunknownn
23. crashandcraveyou likes this
24. addressunknownn reblogged this from apoq
25. unskilled-worker reblogged this from seapuzzle
26. heterofobica likes this
27. islandofatlas reblogged this from seapuzzle
28. bythebed reblogged this from laaaast-hope
29. a-little-black-rain-cloud likes this
30. melissaadamssbitch reblogged this from eat-the-sticker-off-the-apple
31. luciferish reblogged this from patholysis
32. mangeable reblogged this from exites
33. bludgen reblogged this from patholysis
34. in-terdicto reblogged this from laaaast-hope
35. solar-apex likes this
36. h8linmoon reblogged this from thirdeyeblinded

37. laaaast-hope reblogged this from patholysis
38. hence-love-never-fails likes this
39. patholysis reblogged this from eat-the-sticker-off-the-apple
40. patholysis likes this
41. illusnary reblogged this from exites
42. **thirdeyeblinded reblogged this from exites**
43. illusnary likes this
44. unic0rnsandsharks likes this
45. gloomatic reblogged this from exites
46. eat-the-sticker-off-the-apple reblogged this from exites
47. **exites reblogged this from magrittee**
48. xtalrhubarb reblogged this from monolithzine
49. monolithzine reblogged this from t0mbs and added:
    Rene Magritte - The Torturing of the Vestal Virgin
50. thevelvetedge likes this
51. s-a-u-r-o-n reblogged this from apoq
52. malibustacie likes this
53. cynothoglys likes this
54. **genitalya reblogged this from xvst**
55. handysandwich likes this
56. susurrating reblogged this from seapuzzle
57. boogiemouse reblogged this from seapuzzle
58. seapuzzle reblogged this from apoq
59. shredder-senpai reblogged this from apoq
60. the-slug-life-chose-me reblogged this from notpeaches
61. outvisible reblogged this from infestedmeat
62. apoq reblogged this from infestedmeat
63. notpeaches reblogged this from infestedmeat
64. **xvst reblogged this from infestedmeat**
65. banditshawty likes this
66. uako likes this
67. gastly420 reblogged this from infestedmeat
68. **infestedmeat reblogged this from guillotte**
69. cestcoolserieux likes this
70. dancedanceafterdark reblogged this from magrittee
71. moon-apple reblogged this from rumcum
72. sbtrakkt reblogged this from t0mbs
73. ginsoakedboy93 reblogged this from t0mbs
74. nuclearer reblogged this from magrittee
75. feralcattery reblogged this from subwaybum

76. percocet--princess reblogged this from t0mbs
77. skrongpack likes this
78. undeluded reblogged this from t0mbs
79. there-is-no-happy-love reblogged this from magrittee
80. audiophile-psyque reblogged this from magrittee
81. **guillotte reblogged this from t0mbs**
82. rumcum reblogged this from magrittee
83. rawnaldgregoryerickson reblogged this from magrittee
84. **t0mbs reblogged this from magrittee**
85. bptism reblogged this from magrittee
86. subwaybum reblogged this from magrittee
87. soybrain reblogged this from magrittee
88. subwaybum likes this
89. hempbaby reblogged this from magrittee
90. magrittee posted this

The Month of the Grape Harvest (2)

starts off with redundancy
& a table of mnemonic
devices. Anything can be
connected to anything else—
that's an underlying principle
of hermetic semiosis. Any-
thing can be connected; so,
the month finishes with
an occluded view as the
window is hermetically
sealed by an active blockade
of passive lookalikes who
render the shutters redundant.

The Mask of Lightning

Tootooch lived on the
flesh of whales. Mixing
it with cinnamon helped
add the golden tones.

Rod stares down the
Cyclops Queen—will
drinking turmeric in
milk twice a day or

channeling his inner
Lady Gaga help him
most? Gulls fill the skies
from one yellow horizon

to the other. Any pop
star diva would be
jealous. Find all the lines
from this movie which

exist as temporary
royalty in the realm of
the senses. Tomatoes have
lots of anti-oxidants. A

Red Flag warning has
been issued in southwest
Oregon. This is my ball.
My rubber ball. I've had

it for two years. It has
a chemical absorbent to
provide relief & came
to me through a vending

machine at PriceRite,
on NE 2nd Avenue. The
only thing this picture
is missing is an evil face.

Le Cinéma Bleu

The balloon sinks, the
bilboquet floats. Fantômas
is alive & well & working

in a KFC somewhere
near the cinema precinct
south of the Coliseum.

Moonlights as a tourguide.
Day lights up the night.
Nothing is ever what it was.

Le Coup au coeur

Women's power circles
are changing the face
of business. At $220 each
they're pricey; but now
that stainless steel face
can be replaced by any
one of a smorgasbord
of cheap inanimate
objects, whilst a QR code
reveals a previously un-
seen poster for the up-
coming Batman film.

Some things fall by
the wayside as our daily
lives become more &
more digital, but not the
"everyone is a winner"
philosophy so prevalent
in the suburbs or forcing
little girls to wear stiletto
heels whenever they go out
in public. If seeing the pink
of the rose is an illusion,
what's illusory about it?

Act of Violence

The sky is oblong.
The clouds are not.

> Looks more like a
> tremendous explosion
> or a patent leather
> cosmetic makeup
> case. Believe what you
> see not what you are
> told to believe. Graupel
> is not the same as
> hail or ice pellets.

A bell rolls towards
an apartment block.

> Never take the elevator
> when there is no bell
> to push. Too many
> minority students are
> getting suspended. In
> a Native American
> sweat lodge a rapper
> dies. Clenching her
> eyes shut to hold back
> the tears, Kazuko
> rolls onto her side.

The hole in her
stomach seems
larger than
the usual navel.

> She is unaware of
> any missing cargo
> but her breathing rate
> may vary widely. Man-

kind has fought battles
on the sea for more
than 3,000 years. The
rings are banana-
shaped—a metal
bar can put a lot of
pressure on her
skin. Is she the
only person on
earth to have one
eye become larger
than the other
post childbirth?

The New Years

In the closed circles of
psychic apparati, exposed
navels emphasize the
rural-urban rift. It is
from this dark rift that
the winter solstice sun
will emerge, offering
a single world with a
dichotomy of semantics
in which objects co-exist
with primitive types. More
problematic in theory
than in practice, it tends
towards a reductionist
framework. On the day
of the second new moon
after the December solstice
the new years begin.

Merman Hanging from a Gibbet

Harlequin diamonds are
must-haves for fashion-
able women, now that
they are back on the map
for 'it' handbags with new
styles & such modern
colors as Waterlily Pink
& New Bronze available.

& in the home, unpinned,
stuck to the door, access-
orized with the movement
of a hanging merman, they
add a sense of drama &
visual tension to any space.

The Glass Key

for Dashiell Hammett & Jo Nesbø

Ned finds the body of a
Senator's son on the street.
He's tall, lean, mustachioed
& tubercular. He's also
a gambler. & a big fan of
literary noir. You can use
census records & voter
lists to see where he's lived

over the years. They have
a pervasive feeling of moral
& sexual ambiguity which
may not be visible yet be-
cause of a delay in updating
the database. You can also
use them to read about
Harry's journey to Thailand.

The Battle of the Argonne

Jay Gatsby leads
two machine-gun
attachments forward.
Ten of these men, the
most stubborn kind,

gave their last full
measure. The unit, now
at a stall, was saved
by another pigeon.
The only stone road

leading into the forest
went downward for
the central powers.
What does *givry-en-*
argonne mean in English?

Natural Encounters

include

Plenty of opportunities to get up close & personal with concrete countertops & outdoor kitchens.

Discount rates for hotels & motels.

Empowering animals with the ability to make good decisions.

Providing candid photos of female sea turtles nesting.

My perspective on Height Dominance.

Definitions of Common Behavior Terms.

The Leather Elves & other live native New Hampshire animals.

The cutting edge of animal training & presentation with breakfast & lunch included.

Ben Williams, Vice President, who lives in Dorset.

The delicate state of nature.

Your questions that have not been answered.

An adventure through an entire continent.

The way the window on the right has fallen magically & now circles, unsure whether to approach its mate.

La Cascade

This is not the waterfall where
Yoshitsune washed his
horse. It does not flow or fall or
follow through. Is telescopic. In that
the mind is seen in the forest
as well as distant from it.

Tags: california statepark long exposure water

*

A massive earthquake. A tropical cyclone.
A picture of Hokusai. Stochastic acts.

*

He found a shiny object somewhere.
Diane is Betty in the dream . . . she views
her good side as dominant. Irony
abounds. Gloria Swanson says voice
doesn't add anything. Radiohead has
postponed part of its European tour
after a stage collapse in Toronto
killed the band's drum technician.

*

I took many photos of the fall & its pools. The
original one (the first one at night) is a
proof of concept one to show to people
before creating the real one. (Irony defined:
"stated message doesn't equal real message.")
I thought it would be funny to take a picture
of America at war as gasoline prices spike.

*

Alfred Korzybski gave a presentation at a meeting of the American Association for the Advancement of Science in New Orleans where he used the phrase "the map is not the territory." Korzybski used this phrase to mean that people in general do not have access to absolute knowledge of reality, but merely possess a subset of that knowledge that is then tinted through the lenses of their own experience. He further added that it is important for people to know that their understanding of things, "the map," is not a true representation of reality itself or everything represented by reality, or "the territory."

The Upholder of the Law

The elderly mother dresses
down for her new video
in a pair of bright red jeans
& matching lippy. She has
decided her son-in-law
is trying to poison her. The
painful irony is that he is
an Autobot who believes
in upholding the law, but
lacks the firepower to
enforce it. Plus, care &
dignity are wrapped in
so much red tape that they
become safe harbors &
provide immunity from
liability. The new moon
clings to his hat's brim like
a nose ring. Our beautiful
website is coming soon.

The Forest of Paimpont

Sir Lancelot is no
longer available for
interviews &/or photo
opportunities due to the
new set of contractual
obligations he's entered
into. From here on in
it's Murdoch & the
Morgans—J.P., le Fey—
you'll be crossing swords
with. From here on in
it's Getty & 20th Century
Fox for rights & royal-
ties. This image,
taken just before he
entered La Forêt de
Paimpont for a final
time, is the last left
in the public domain, a
reminder that chevalry
is not always chivalrous.

The Adulation of Space (2)

He felt happy & pain-free only
on stage, immersed in his music.
String Theory & the Geometry of
Hydroponic Strawberries. Listen
to, download, play & stream the

song. The elders only smile sadly.
I've bought eight t-shirts from
this guy. Californian worshippers
chose blindfolds. There is scepticism
in the mainstream media. Luxury

limousines drove up the stairs.
I have his posters on my wall. Will
he be able to go back to the boy
band life? Don't forget to watch *A*
Thousand Kisses, Episode 37. In the

blank space alongside the photograph,
an anonymous letter-writer had
scribbled a shocking & hate-filled
message. Does it bother you that ten-
nis doesn't get that kind of adulation?

Youth Illustrated

Now that reality shows
have developed some
          sort of deep metaphysical
connection with live-action
          games where players
dress up in costume &
          get involved in areas
derived from the Greek
like weapon trajectory
          calculations & image
processing, renting
Camelot on DVD &
singing along with it
          just doesn't register
any more. The competition
to narrow down the
          pool is heating up—
not the contestant pool
but the wannabe guest
judges all dressed
          up & running behind
the circus trucks.

La Malédiction

When run through any
Icelandic-English
translation app, the
atomic hypothesis &
its concept of cloud comes
out resembling a gothic
horror screen-play. No
consideration for classical
theory. No sensitivity
toward sociological
phenomena. Persons
under the age of 18 are
included only if they
play in a marching band
or Drum & Bugle Corps.

The Drop of Water

A microchip im-
plant is placed
under the skin.

Nicotine patches
are spread upon
it. A free hand

selection tool that
includes an inter-
active game is

used to specify
the region of inter-
est. Whether that

be the mechanics
of water or the
flow of mythology

begin by drawing
a circular object
on your canvas.

Megalomania

No-one questions the
usefulness of having
a power generator
around the house. A-

pocalypse obsession
goes back a long way,
& any highly-descriptive
formalism with reasoning

features is convenient for
developing an ontology
of practical steps to re-
store humanity. It becomes

what the world offers it.
Little bits of coloured glass.
Or. Walking the sweltering
streets of Manhattan naked.

Pom 'po pom 'po pon po pon pon

La vache quit rit
& les lapins
qui jouent des
tambours have
little in common
except that Magritte
called this his
vache period &
painted lots of
rabbits—& other
animals—during it.

But, there goes the
neighborhood now
that musicians
have moved in next
door, & everybody
knows, as Leonard
Cohen reminds us,
that musicians fuck
like . . . well, like
rabbits. So, pom 'po,
paradiddle. Pom 'po,
paradise lost. Pon
po pon pon paradox.

Mental Complacency

My grandfather was
a technician for Ma
Bell. He said, "We are

complacent in our
color attributions. The
only way to receive a

signal is to eliminate the
noise. There are no co-
incidences, merely portals."

The Amorous Vista

Without this inter-
vening presence
of a sudden &
aggressive getaway

with some significant
other to that highly
recommended place
to karaoke, then it's

essentially a bucolic
image, even if no
sheep, no alpacas,
no fertility-symbols,

no Lacoste alligators
mingling with angels
holding dynamite, no
animated cuddly lions,

no eggs or rabbits, no
Japanese women,
no cameo appearance
from Don Quixote.

Faraway Looks

Drained of context,
of creative market
mechanisms &
public policy, the
interior surface of
the shell is contoured.
Perhaps an actor sits
there knitting. The
mechanical, despite
its notion of longevity,
is just the biological
on a shorter rope—
banality was never
intended for posterity.
History is historical
romance, politics is
science fiction, to
quote Foucault. Work-
place romance
is a local construct.

Fortune Telling

Someone
opened a
door & let
me see the
future. It
was as
bland as
the present
& as blind
as the past.

A double cypher

The operation is a calligram. It
is a mark of ill-breeding to use
French phrases or words unless
they're resting on a floor made safe
& visible by its own coarseness.

All this litter on the ground —
ask for an explanation. The
calligram has a triple role.
The vague uneasiness pro-
voked is a Cuban gentleman.

Severely censure the habit of
using sentences which admit
of a double meaning. We have
evidence of failure & its ironic
remains. Augment the alphabet.

Splintered wood, fragmented
shapes. Many men can converse
on no other subject than their
every day employment. Words
can no longer be reconstituted.

Sources:
This Is Not a Pipe, by Michel Foucault
The Ladies' Book of Etiquette (1860), by Florence Hartley

Blood Will Tell

Even when
refurbished
to incorporate
beautiful en-

suites or worn
with denim
for a smart
casual style

property derived
from things from
nature is a step
back in time.

La Courbure de l'univers

Light, which
normally travels
in straight
lines, follows

a curved path
when affected by
gravity. This is a
serious bottle.

The Secret Life II

Economics is boring. So
too are all those Star
Wars toys when / they're
kept in the box. & boring

is why even the live
bad man black dog bite
mix of Henry Kissinger
as he mounts his return

to Hollywood is now
available in French for
free. How else to explain
the media visibility of

Chaos theory with its
streaming versions of old
cell phones being tossed
into the trash? Beauty is

uncovered in the most
surprising of subjects—
the discovery of a new
food, a detailed snap-shot

of online teen behavior—
but the *duende* is too fragile
to survive by scraping algae
from the rocks upon which

they live. The pressure to
perform prevents proteins
from being made. Every
poem is the story of itself.

Spiritual Exercises

Begin by dismantling the
self. Taking things apart
is fascinating. A first
pivotal step is the right
hemisphere of the brain;
is tagged with Hamlet,
madness, melancholy;
includes coral, jelly fish,
anemones. The colors
of the actual products
will look slightly different
in reproduction. A
character map is free on
all Windows machines.

A Courtesan's Palace

The unicorn has
left his horn
in the anteroom.
It is a courtesy.

Besides. Some
things are better
left unsaid. She
took her face off.

The Great War I

Unlike, say, the Gaelic
for *kiss my ass*, most
Declarations of In-
dependence are top-

heavy with awkward
or extremely dated
references. Some-
times they present

as an organic synthe-
sizer, a Granny Smith
apple perhaps, with a
sound set restricted

to industrial use
because of extremely
mixed reviews. At
other times as an

holistic framework
that purports to look
at all aspects of life
as spiritual practice

but then recommends
the confining of women
to the home & the use
of tanks to shell densely

populated areas. Colon-
ialism is a patriarchal
system. The methods
devour themselves.

The Great War II

Sometimes she con-
fuses words that
sound alike. Such as.
Violets & violence.

So. She thinks the
soldiers are off
picking flowers.
Have brought some

to her. She goes
out walking to show
them off. Back to
the sea. Dressed

for. All in white.
Morning. Her face the
color of violence. Some-
times she confuses

words. Not always.
Life is a parasol.

Le Grand Siècle

Pick a point in time
& stick a pin in it.

Attach a piece of string,
50 or 100 years long.

An area defined, ob-
long in a circle's arc.

Three sides with forest
lining them. A low

block wall across the
other. In front of which

a faceless avatar being
stared at by a windowless

mansion. Grass underfoot.
A plaster ceiling overhead.

Deadening the acoustics. A
silent century. How grand.

The Wonders of Nature

One of the
wonders of
nature is its
ability to re-
use objects
over & over

in similar
or disparate
settings &
make them
new again.
So, once

more a ship,
the waves,
the very sea
shore, on which
a pair of stone-
crossed lovers.

La Pipe

```
                pipe
Surely          a
Magritte    not
can see     is
that    this
```

The Apparition (2)

They're keywords. That
much he recognizes
even if he doesn't
recognize the discipline
that they come from. "The
labels could mean any-
thing," he thinks. Which
means. He carries one
himself. Or two. He doesn't
think. Which means.
He isn't. He appears.
Walking towards
one of two horizons.
Which means. They
may not be.

The Survivor

That was the year
we wintered in
Montparnasse. The
ferry, I remember,
was empty apart
from us, might never
have sailed except
its skipper lived
on the other side
of the river & she
wanted to get
home that night. Up-
stream was thick
with forest. There
were fireworks
somewhere. I heard
them, but I did not
see their bloom.

Applied Dialectics

thesis

       poetry

antithesis

       war

synthesis

       woetry

The Light-Breaker

History is. Typhoon.
The Bay of Bengal.

Ship washed up. Large.
Left there. Broken down

by locals. Scrap, metal,
parts to use. Such

plenitude never seen
before. New industry.

Now stretches for many
kilometers along the

beaches of Bangladesh.
Pollution prevails. Most

things done by hand or
not much more advanced.

Small men or children
in narrow passageways.

What air there is is
full of toxins. Is death.

Is dangerous. Is life.
Is nothing else to do.

The countryside destroyed.

*

Breaking lights is different.

Is still to do with ships.
Broken down. Small parts

of them. Collected. Port-
holes. Filled with sky

or sometimes emptiness.
Is clean. Is dirty. Distance.

The Promised Land (2)

Short-range ordered
nanoholes can
improve the health
of rice farmers &
consumers or even,
with the addition
of the new bad-boy
vibe, form a picture of
a dying Michael Jackson
that's part solid, part
liquid. Such prototyping,
with its specially de-
signed cells & the use
of heat sinks, would
seem to be an inbuilt
aspect of our human
software; but the only
constant factor in
natural phenomena
is universal change —
a life-size figurative
re-enactment of da
Vinci's *Last Supper*
made from wax just
doesn't cut it as a
wonder of the world.

The Automaton

No cat to
bell, but
the grelot
keeps on
mindless-
ly looking
for one.

The Literal Meaning IV

Sad woman. Is
not. Is neither.

Men falling from
the sky, rosaries

of stars, a castle
in the Pyrenees,

transparency, a
fence of sentinels

or sentiment, win-
dows which are

mirrors of the soul.
Were not. Were

never. All is allusion.

The Spy

The premise of Sun Tzu's *The Art of Espionage*, a prequel written to cash in on the runaway success of *The Art of War*, is that though the world of Espionage obeys the rules of Heaven, the life force of the individual spy is, *a priori*, out of balance.

A posteriori, how they end up is governed by which principle holds sway within them. Too much yin & the spy may be consumed by elements of self-destruction, display a subconscious desire to be outed, manifest it through actions such as dressing up as Gérard Depardieu in drag & living their life entirely in the dark. Too much yang & they become spy-hunter, keyhole peeper, closet cannibal, turning on their own, seeing them as enemy equal to those on the opposing side.

It's a precursor to the classic predator / prey model later postulated by both Lotka & Volterra, with the ratio of yin to yang determining who is x & y in the differentiated equation. But this is a finite model with an endpoint of zero. Too much egocentricity, too much paranoia. It does not stop when all known spies have been consumed; there must be others out there. Trust no-one, not even oneself. Eliminate them all.

Meditation

Buddham saranam gacchāmi

Photo editing software. Someone sporting riding breeches. Retailer-perceived brand equity. Guides to the different stages of German intellectual development. Visual parallels made between the use of pesticides & degradation of the land. An exodus of female talent. A problem assuming added significance in view of rapid globalization. Temporal logics. Improper drainage. You need to upgrade your Flash Player.

Dhammam saranam gacchāmi

Steel doesn't protect sugar farmers. Nothing was found today during a search in South Carolina for missing Chili teenager Brittanee Drexel. Optical signals affected by an external magnetic field. The fringe that consumes. Size 34B Black with silver sequins, silver beads & silver beaded trim. Policy endogeneity. A neckline like that would be bad for makeup. What does it cost? Sort it out monkey nuts!

Sangham saranam gacchāmi

Nothing has proven to be better than this song. Eliminating artificial lighting. The strip-searching of women in Australian prisons. Price competition produces mixed results. Clothing that is all natural & free of toxins. Large as the executions arrive. Lighting a fire. An embroidered osteopath. A trance duo based in the U.S.A. Common bugs can freeze the machine. Is there any way to make my chest look bigger?

> *I go for refuge in the Buddha.*
> *I go for refuge in the Dharma.*
> *I go for refuge in the Sangha.*

Discourse on Method (2)

In there for
show, or
core co-
ordinate?
Descartes —
bald, be-
spectacled,
but not at all
bewildered
by the juxta-
position of
the box &
horse's bell
Magritte has
placed be-
fore him.

To him
two objects
in Euclidian
space; a three-
dimensional
definition
makes all
things
relative.

Quand l'heure sonnera

Venus de
Milo, hot-
air balloon,
sky/sea/sand —
writing down
the elements
doesn't have
the tension
of a painterly
arrangement

unless you
know the sub-
text. So. Some
clues. Start
with a child-
hood incident.
Continue with
de Chirico.

Souvenir de voyage II

There was a sea-
side somewhere,
but nowhere near
the sea. We walked
along it, kicking
at rocks, ignoring
strangers until
they'd passed. "Who
was that masked
man?" I asked.

Perspective: David's Madame Récamier (2)

Assume a life-
line in reverse.

Death comes first.
Before that, head-

stone, interment,
mourning crowd,

laying out, the prep-
aration of the body.

Move forwards.
Miss Marx. Pass

through two
revolutions, a liberal

monarchy, literary
salons. Chateaubriand,

Mme de Staël amongst
the names. Napoleon.

Bring in Ingres, who
uses Magritte's posed

figure as basis for
La Grande Odalisque.

Which influences
David. Who does not

finish his painting
of Madame Récamier.

Was pissed when told
that someone else was

getting the commission.
But starts it anyway.

The Master of the Revels

In *Il Casanova* di Federico
Fellini, a giant head of Venus
begins to emerge from the
Grand Canal. Set in the
rural French countryside,
the factory by the side of
the lake is small; but still
lives undergo critical changes
as water & land are con-
taminated. The head rises
creakily to eye level & a
cable breaks. I have an idea
that the ideal drop is equal
to the length of your leg. In
his infancy Pindar was fed
honey by bees as an augury
of supreme eloquence. The
crowd cheers as the master
of the revels extols the
goddess of love. Learn
to control that one footed
wobble & you'll find things
a whole lot easier. This page
contains notes I have been
collecting on walking the slack
wire. Much of it is contradictory.

The Fountain of Youth

Last seen in
the Pyrenees.

Perched on a
peak. Small in

context but
omnipotent.

Now wraps its
wings around

a reed. Petrified.
Monumental.

Fashionable People

Autumn is a tricky time.
Fashionistas get ready to
face the cold winter months
but try not to completely let
go of their summer styles.
Judgey blondes, with little
to qualify them beyond
starpower, must practise

soothsaying &/or augury
in order to keep coming
out of the woodwork with
new lifestyle brands that we
must either consume or else
opt out of the fashion stream.

The Domain of Arnheim (1949)

A sudden snap
freeze shatters the

window, but not
the bird outside.

Inside is a different
story; though on &

in reflection much
the same. Some play

on words that can't
exist in the original.

Le Rendez-Vous

Smallish mongoose; pointed
face; solitary, in pairs or small
groups. Slightly diminishing
the polar distance. The history
teacher lectured us every day,
did not sacrifice the quality
of her scorn for speed, her words
at first awakened horror but
continued abuse became mere
recitation. Something about a
dead horse, diurnal floggings.

The Cape of the Tempests

Spring in the
Southern Ocean.

Caliban is off
looking for wood.

The rock moves
closer to the sleeper.

He is dreaming
of Helen Mirren.

Rose & Pear

Snap an index finger
onto the skull. Make
a loud, drumming
noise. The subsequent
sine wave flatlines
even though the signal
is strictly limited at the
threshold. Ear drops &
finger rings rebound.
The floral bergamot
finish lingers for lovely
effect. It begins to rain.

La Fissure

The earth opens up.
Money appears,
U.S. dollars. Some
change hands, the

rest remain in open
view, available to
anyone. A teaser?
Or a smoking gun?

What was. What
is. An open window
able to bend light
in both directions.

Le Pain Quotidien

If the visibility is
good, & you're on
top of something

like the Tokyo Tower,
then the city's most
beloved retro icon

might be seen main-
taining her exposure
to cloud-based apps.

The Art of Living

The orange people
used to be every-
where. Now only
a few scattered centers
are left. All small,
except, of course, for
Donald Trump, the
center of the universe,

with his swollen head
& disconnected brain.
The body transformed
by a business suit; but his
face still stained from the
clothes he wore before.

The Chamber of the Barley

It's a natural cycle. The
bird waits for the snow
to melt, for the water to
irrigate the land, for the
grain to grow, to ripen.

Then it swoops down, to
gorge. We hide in a cave, &
wait for the bird to find its
fullness, to retreat to its peak,
replete, to wait through winter.

A Friend of Order

The urge to analyze Magritte
has proved hard to resist.
Praising creative work is im-
portant: people need to feel
as if their work matters. A seg-
ment of the literature drawn
from the point of contact.

Most mornings I listen to the
BBC on my way to work, hear
how Pretty Boy Floyd has finally
been captured in one of the
vaults of the Chapelle Notre Dame
de Lourdes. Even as a young
girl, she had an urge to run.

The Key to Dreams (1935)

The horse ≠ the door,
the clock ≠ the wind,
the jug ≠ the bird. But —
unless, of course,
something is lost in
translation — the valise =
the valise. So, open it
up, put in, in any order,

horse, door, clock, wind,
jug, & bird so that, out of
sight, they won't bother you
any more, & close. Open
the other valise & put
the first in that. Shut tight.

Georgette at the Piano

Just as my brushes on
a canvas make music,
so, too, more precisely,
does Georgette at her

chosen instrument. Desire
is put aside. Outside of
this room, yes; but here
the keyboard & her hands

are sharp areas of paint,
of color. Contiguous; &
only Arnold Schoenberg
could make music out of

the separate elements. But
here is where I hope to have
the magic to bring it all to-
gether, to put music into.

La Grande Marée

Bells   Winter snows, the
                sleighbells. Broken ice
                in the river. Parallax
                measurements. How
                people navigated &
                predicted the weather
                by watching meteors.

clouds   A small card with
                the cloud template is
                saturated with a deep
                affection. I already
                have the silver wing
                in heartgold. It will
                soon stop raining
                in the mountains.

& sky   Clouds & small bells
                falling from the sky. A-
                mazing sea born water-
                falls that appear as the
                tides recede. Rocks left
                outside the frame.

& tides   Computational power has
                led us to revisit the
                canonical tidal model.

The Orchestra Conductor

It is self-
hypnotism
without the
watch. It is
surrealism
without
the apple. Dis-

daining Mesmer
disdaining
Magritte I
play Miles'
Time after Time
time after time
trying to

convince the
day to move
to a place
where I can
watch my hands
dance & dance
along with them.

L'Aube à Cayenne (1)

The transition to full horti-
culture comes at a cost. A
six-hour flight, custom-built
containers, the whole year
as a graph where the darker

blue shadings represent the
twilight phases. Vasectomy
is less risky. Advancements
in robotics plus a coordinated
script have demonstrated good

outcomes—complete health
solutions controlled by the
human mind & tailored to go
the distance once mining be-
gins again at the Space Center.

The Face of Genius

This is taken from René
Magritte's ninth mixtape,
carrying on from, but a long
time after, his 16th century album,
*The Perfect Pairing to Your Skin-
care Products*, still remembered
fondly for its dramatic dub
version of the strangling of
Philip II, then Metropolitan
of Moscow, later sanctified.

Bather

Despite the curves she is straight line defined. With *feng shui* you learn how to place things so that the energy flows. She is facing the door. The sea needs a mirror on the horizon to replicate what she sees.

Portrait d'Eluard

Eluard used
to write *to*
write on the

body of his
wife. Then
Dalí came a-

long & wrote
off into the
sunset on her.

The Art of Conversation IV

Though each is in some way
present here, the swans are

unaware of Arnold Böcklin, or
Rachmaninoff, or the more

contemporary William Carlos
Williams, even though all three

overlap in time, in linked rings
just like the ones the swans are

swimming in as they contend in
a sea which love partly encloses.

The Endearing Truth

Wine, bread, apples, & a
question of perception. What
stands out? The alcoves or
the painted table? The text-
ured wall? So. Focus on the
contents. Discard the bread
& wine — they're simply tricks
of a trade. Then wonder why

there are no fishes. Were
there ever any or does their
replacement by the apples re-
write the parables? Does this
miraculous piece of *trompe l'oeil*
infer there were no miracles?

Le Beau Ténébreux

Fantômas is back in town.

His penchant for masquerade is
informed by a close reading of
sermons using hermeneutic methods.

He asks for a room at the
back, not the front of the hotel.

His conception of history & geology
comes from mass-produced fictional
texts that are in transmedia circulation.

He decides to change his clothes.

He told a newspaper. "I've no ex-
perience working with multi-colored
bulbs. My favorite was Harrison Ford
on the plane. I love Harrison Ford."

He stood up for an America
staying quiet but largely
fueled by basic research
into cell biology & renewed
interest in lipid research.

He hides within his hat.

Modern

A straight line between
those two points in
Euclidean space shows
it is a second head of

the damsel in this (white)
dress that stares out from
the backseat of her town car
at the more fully-fleshed

version of herself. The eco-
nomic crisis has hit hard.
There is falling demand
for everything from office

space to orders for time
machines. The pavement
is too costly to repair.
Her feet sink into it. Else-

where the moon is green.

Heartstring

I look at this
& immediately
think: *my cup
runneth over*. &
then I think: *with*

*clouds? Things
with little sub-
stance to them
except in stormy
weather?* I look

at this again &
think that the
painting is no-
thing more than
a (center)piece

of flimsical whim-
whammery, a
sorbet glass
posed in a post-
card pastoral

setting that is just
too picture-per-
fect. I look at this
again & think: *this
makes me think.*

La Fin du Monde

He followed the travel
guide carefully, replacing the
            listed sites of interest with
the actual objects when he
            found them. Houses that
had a history, a row of shops,
            fountains, parks, the plaza
      with its famous wall of shame.
Once he had the scene he could
            fill it with inhabitants, just as
the book did when it decorated
            cathedral ceilings or described
the inside of a hall. Otherwise
            façades, or acts of stagecraft.
Walls that flickered into being
as he approached & hid what-
            ever lay behind. He saw the
      railway station & walked to-
wards it. Climbed up the steps
            to find it was the concourse
where the world came to an end.

La Page Blanche (2)

Centrifugal
in that it has
a center &
words fly
in all directions.

Gravitational
in that the
words are drawn
towards the center
as they cohere.

During &
after. There is
no such thing
as a blank page.

The Life of Insects

Not some-
thing she really
cared about;
but global warming
was drying
up all the
hotpools, & this
was the only
one left, the last
chance to
immerse herself
in a lifestyle
she had always
been frightened of
but wanted to
try before
it died.

Une panique au moyen âge

for Kirsten Kaschock

Exuberance
is in an eye

      much more be-
      holden to the

magic of the
moment than

      to the pattern
      of the dance.

Reflections of Time

Emerged from
a spell of writing *A*
to the *Q* of an
email interview.
One unexpected
outcome was a

change in the type-
face I'd been using.
Used to be Verdana —
now it's Palatino
Linotype. If you
can't give your

words historical
importance then
the least you can
do is to make
them look a little
more attractive.

Prince Charming

This piece is / a note on this piece.

She found it unicorned inside the
hiding-place of those animals
that did not make it onto the Ark.

The Evening Gown

I am going through a lean
period. Words do not
make sense or hang
together the way they
should. At night I watch

the stars. They should be
easy to describe. A single
word, a simple phrase.
Instead they are all the
same even though I give

them separate names.
Thousands die by day.
They all have the same
name. Famine & firefights
in countries that were once

romantic, that poets passed
through on their way to
somewhere else. I read a-
bout them even though the
words do not make sense,

run together in a way they
should never do. Stars
do not come out. I give
the spaces separate names.
They are all anonymous.

Le Sourire du Diable

Oedipus might feel intimi-
dated. A giant keyhole,
a tiny key. But that's
what happens when you
run home to Mother, no
matter whether she's
the legendary subject
of a da Vinci portrait

or the restoration of an
earlier restoration of a
heavy prog band out of
Germany, known for the
completely self-referential
songs of the female lead.

[...not only to read the text &
to look at the pictures but to
fill the gap between the two
with meaning — that is, to
produce a plausible fiction
that will relate them — then
the key is to the keyhole as
the text is to the pictures.]
Alain Robbe-Grillet:
La Belle Captive

A Poster Project for the Affiliated Unions of Belgian Textile Workers

Myra was tempted into the milieu of the
sub-prime mortgage. World capitalism
went into meltdown. Crisis resolution
has since become extremely complex.

Grim door Of war

The Flowering Dogwood is some-
times treated as a separate genus.
Shuttles are often made of wood
from the Flowering Dogwood.
Climb a bell tower to get up close.

For it was the war-time work

The filling yarn is carried through the
shed of warp yarns to the other side
of the loom by finger-like carriers called
rapiers. A rapier loom is a shuttleless
weaving loom, bending the political system
at the center of the world economy.

Of the women Of the Brussels Lace Committee

Mule spinners' cancer is caused by the
prolonged action of mineral oils on
the skin of the scrotum. Shale oil was
deemed to be the most carcinogenic.

That opened the way to me.

From 1911 to 1938, there were 500
deaths amongst cotton mule spinners
but only three amongst wool mule
spinners. How could sub-prime
mortgages going sour turn into an
aging population of skilled women?

Bobbin.

A stationary package of yarn is used to
supply the weft yarns in the rapier machine.

Landscape

This was the year the
samba arrived in *La
Côte d'Azur*. Fashionably

late, as befits a traveler
with either a load of
baggage & a room to go

to, or else with just a
parasol & a promised
place beneath the palms.

The Beneficial Promise

Psychological research confirms the
headline that the trillions of beneficial
bacteria already in our intestines will
strengthen privacy protections for
the digital age. Not all such antipoverty
efforts hit their mark; but down-home
adages such as "real maple syrup
shows promise in protecting brain
health," when combined with the
original concepts of kindergartens,
reflect a truth in human development.

L'okapi

If he truly loves the woman
he must wear *anneaux ronds*
torsadés en laiton oxidé in a
section of town that still shows

fleeting moments of animal
behavior. It's a weathered,
crumbling place, made all
the more magnificent by

trackless centuries filled
with polished pop & striking
synths, & the towering masses
of the Virunga volcanoes.

A Taste of The Invisible (1927)

In this world of billions, we are
told that the entire global
economy essentially boils down
to just two idealized people, a
buyer & a seller. True theology

is not about the mistaken road
or a cold evening in cardboard
boxes. Think fresh pear, allocate
taste descriptors—sweet, bitter,
ripe, crunchy, peppery—but

any of those terms can equally
be applied to many other unseen
things. Macro or micro, there is a
commonality—once out of sensory
range, all things become invisible.

The Postcard

Chère Georgette

The apple is full, & almost ready
for eclipse. But the UV rays it
gives off are intense, & I've been
exposed to an overdose of them,
simply by going out onto the balcony
to see if the eclipse has started yet.

I should be wearing a hat, but
a bowler is not the easiest thing to
have on all the time. Maybe I should
have bought one of those embroidered
baseball caps that Donald Trump gets
around in & brought it with me. With
a different message, though. Nothing
as gauche & inviting hubris as his
hat has. Something simple, apt. Like
`"un objet rencontre son image."`

Ton mari
René

Les objets d'art de René Magritte

a pair of diamante lorgnettes

birds that are birds, that are not birds, that are, sometimes, something
    else

clouds stolen from the opening of *The Simpsons*

death masks

Edgar Allan Poe

Fantômas

Georgette. Naked Georgette. Clothed Georgette. Incomplete Georgette.
    Always Georgette

horses' bells

inflamed euphoniums

jokes & jockeys

kiss. No, not the rock group but the Rodin sculpture. But not the Rodin
    sculpture, only the space it fills

lost worlds

Martin Luther & the King of the Jews

neologism, or at least the attachment of new labels

open-toed boots

pleasure that the girl gets from eating a bird

quantum leaps

rendering the impossible possible

sacks that cover the lovers' heads

this is not an apple, nor a pipe, not even a piece of cheese

using speech to show how speech misleads

victory is what was hoped for in this break in the clouds, even if they
    turned their backs on the war & the victory came unseen

what lasts is how the lovers shared a space, not how they looked at one
    another

x-rays of leaves, the skeletons of trees

"Your dialectics & your Surrealism *en plein soleil* are threadbare," wrote
    André Breton

    "Sorry, Breton, but the invisible thread is on your bobbin," replied
    Magritte

Zeus. Anger. Hubris

La robe de l'aventure

Dermochelys coriacea, the
leatherback turtle, does not
have a carapace, looks
like an overgrown okra
pod with flippers & fins,
but is the only thing that
gives this scene the marine
setting it probably is.
                    Other-
wise is floating in the air,
above a drowned *inconnue*
who is / likewise out of
water as well as in it, out-
stretched on a beach &
reaching up with her dancer's
arms to form the mammal
shape which has substance
only after passing by them.

The Domain of Arnheim (2)

It was Ellison who suggested they were prognostic of death.
Edgar Allan Poe: *The Domain of Arnheim*

Magritte's love for Poe is
elsewhere evidenced by
a painting titled after the
Imp of the Perverse, &
the appearance of Arthur
Gordon Pym on the mantel-
piece in *Not to be Reproduced*.

One of each of those; but
this is one of nine variants —
oil or gouache — that has
the same title, painted across
twenty-eight years. Not to
mention the guest appearance
of the eagle & its nest in

several other paintings. Some
doubt about the date of this
version. I like to think was done
near the end of the artist's life.
May not be true but there are
clues. A candle to light the way,
& the way the bird is poised as

if for take-off, tearing itself out
of a landscape it does not want
anyone else's hand laid upon.

The Village of the Mind

is the product of medical
science, manifested in its
purest shape when a disease
is new. This introduction
of a virulent organism has
been depicted as a triangle
consisting of two episodes
of new millennium TV &
a contemporary yet timeless
glass & metal occasional

furniture range that displays
many of the empirical phe-
nomena associated with
predator-prey relationships.
Global extinction forces
languages to change. The
world's population of in-
sect pollinators is nearing a
critical point. Not even time
to lay out the winding sheets.

Force of Habit

The sky flies
behind a gilded
bird inside a
cage which sings
imprisoned in
an apple. *Und
so weiter*; until
one hits the wall

the painting is
fixated on. &
then the house
outside of which
the painter. No-
thing else is real.

The Finery of the Storm

Since many of the big
    players these days
        are using AI to boost
        customer loyalty &
    subsequent revenue,
it's not surprising

            that every guitarist,
        at some point, has
    their sound modified
    by a distortion gen-
        erated by an area
            of machine learning.

The Revealing of The Present

The present is a house that
has only windows. A thin
roof. No rooms. The sun
is cut in half by a cloud
passing across its face, re-

calling Buñuel. Is that a
pond with flowers in it? I
walk down to pick some,
carry them inside. The past is
a finger testing &/or tasting

the light. Elsewhere a cloud
passes across the moon. The
present is a vase of flowers in-
side a house surrounded by a
garden made foggy by autumn.

Memory (2)

The apple has
   rolled down the
      bas-relief & left a
         stain. Or maybe the
            sculpture has wept
            tears of blood &

            dried them with
           the apple. I can't
      recall what really
   happened. Perhaps
a sip of water might
refresh my memory.

Le Palais des Souvenirs

This hotel should be shut down.
Blood keeps dripping on to

the bathroom floor, so much
of it it spills over & stains the

mesa which it rides above. A
man in a car outside our rooms

plays Mexican music at high
volume until well after mid-

night. When I complain, he
brings me funeral flowers.

Popular Panorama

Escheresque. Is there
such a word? The top
definition of *crapaud*,
a word characterized by

explorations of infinity,
architecture, & tessel-
lation, is toad or frog.
Jigsaw pieces as far as

the eye can see. Each
is folded in half & the
folded edges are placed
together. Hidden in

the basement, remixed
with a forest, & topped by
the sea. Visible from a t-
shirt. Fit for a paradox.

La Part du Feu

In no particular
order, the clues are
a carrot, an egg, &
a glass of some un-
known liquid, *vin*
or vinegar, it's not
clear. In no particular
order, raindrops keep
falling from the ceil-

ing, a candle halos
but provides no light —
though an external
light source casts a
compressed shadow
of the housekeeper on
to the carpet. In no part-
icular order, Hercule
Poirot, as played by

David Suchet —who
isn't — is dead, the
housekeeper main-
tains not a vigil but
a pretense of life
within the room, hard
to tell if the egg is
hard-boiled, easy to
see the detective isn't.

The Discovery of Fire (3)

```
a bass horn catches alight
a bass hor    atches a  gh
a bas  h r     tc es a   g
   bas  h       c es
    as  h         es
```

Wreckage of the Shadow (1)

Renaissance is alive &
thriving this year. No-
thing else to touch it for
style or energy. Disassembled
birds—hallucinatory, peri-

lous as a minefield—set
faces to grimace, then set
out to create epic doom
metal albums from flat
unpolished non-metal

surfaces that carry no
images of the world
around yet still reflect
the importance of set-
ting up a *mise-en-scène*.

The Connivance (2)

Today was the
day I'd put aside
for Patagonian tooth-
fish, but overfishing
by illegal longliners
has rendered them
commercially extinct

so all I can
do now
is cast
some
short
lines
into

the ocean & re-
mind them they
probably would have
lasted longer if
they'd continued
to be known as
Chilean Sea Bass.

Total: 0

     Having been told that
  the next digital revolution
      would come about by
   finding a cornerstone to

     act as a key to decode
    your name, then trans-
       posing those numbers
   onto your face so as to

   explore your relationship
      with your spirit animal,
    Magritte tried it out &
    came up with nothing.

[Untitled]

We have seen parts
of this before. The

sleeper in his capsule
hotel, dreams keeping

him suspended above
a familiar meteorite

from which the
landscape stays its

distance, in thrall to
the gravitational pull.

The Art of Living

The rave was all that
was promised. Music in
various colors, smoke
of various sorts, a
subsequent disconnect

between limbs & mind —
while at the same time
both feel amazingly
intertwined. Living in
La La Land isn't
art, it is artifice.

The Silvered Chasm

The e-library   charges
me $42 for   a 24 hour
pass to access   any
single steam   punk
novel. They   do not
usually take   me
long to read;   but
this one has   a serious
tension to it,   that boils
its way to eat   my walls
away. It melts   crowbars, has
peeled the eyes   from the jester
bilboquets & left   them pasted
to a nearby   plinth. The now
revealed bells   ring out in
horror. I can   not look
away. The   steampunk novel
remains unfinished   reading. $42
PayPalled for   another day.

The Song of the Sirens

I am waiting for the Prince
of Ithaca to pass by. My

weapons for the skirmish are
lined up behind me. A glass

of water to wet the throat
should stronger singing

be required. The candle is a
lighthouse in reverse, as an

attraction not a warning. A
leaf to augment the wreath.

The stone wall to keep me up-
right when he embraces me.

(Untitled Collage, c. 1926)

Eyeballs drone across the
sky at regular intervals.
Occasionally they fall. Still
see nothing. Or, if they do,
it does not register. The

bird on wings of song has
escaped its cage, lies flat
upon a table. A 1920s
flapper thinks the cage is
an apartment block, looks

for an empty one to live in.
The sky is a sandy shade
of ambergris. It may not be a
bird. Whales swim by. They
sing. In an unknown register.

L'Écuyère

There's a nursery rhyme I part
remember. Something about
riding a cock-horse to Banbury
Cross, to see a fine lady upon
a white horse. Perhaps that's
what's happening here. The
young girl, now dismounted
from her mother's knee, has
turned her back on the white
horse & the lady in — though
clothed — Godiva pose. Is per-
haps contemplating the cubism
of the tombstone that her body
has become, the tumbled straight-
edged landscape, the upright
dwellings, the church beyond.
Is that Banbury Cross? she may
be wondering. Which way is the
lady facing as she rides along?

Oasis

The stillness of death
ranges over this vast
plain. I am at a cross-
road in my contiguous
physical map; any
therapy seems only
to have adverse effects.

The shape of the time
interval is less recogniz-
able, imposes limitations
on the raster & vector
datasets already open for
business just across the
street from the condo

development. 95% of
all cats will become
ecstatically attached to
any thing hollow or over-
hanging. Whole kernel
corn right out of the
can is a treat for catfish.

Le Coeur du Monde

~~Five~~ Four
unicorns. One
died in the
making of
this piece
of the poem.

*

Later he read
to her. She
listened
in braille. Λ
unicorn caught
its horn in
the holes
on the page
& broke its
neck trying
to get free.

*

No primer, so
eventually
the beta
carotene bled
through the
whitewash. Nothing
so sad as a
donkey with
a carrot on its
head at a $75º$
angle while
its dick
hangs limp.

*

One
unicorn left.
One unique horn.

*

In & of it-
self unaugmented; but
the box it comes
in is quite decorative.
&, anyway, there is
always something
striking about
a dead unicorn.

Collage (1966) (1)

hand / men / curtain

one of the best
hairstyles a man
could sew by hand
was a hypocrite of
great proportions

curtain / sphere / sea

embellish your window
treatments with a clown
fish & a sea anemone, or a
symbiotically bound glass
collection from west elm

men / sea / sphere

Nine geometricall exercises,
for young sea-men, &
others that are studious. I
knew it behoved me to
drop at once. Far below me.

sphere / hand / sea

keep starboard (green)
NGOs are acting as subjects
of a global institutional culture
the dino sphere is the novelty
bio-kit of the future

Le Musée du Roi

The man is the night-
light left on to make the
dark seem less fright-
ening. He is outlining
a way through or, may-
be, a way out. All it
takes is an oversized
horse's bell; is used as
balance, needs a granite
block wall to rest upon.

*

The hills stretch away
in rows, into the blue,
each row a different
degree of darkness, on
one of which, neither
fore- nor background,
sits a château. It is the
only man-made thing
contained within the
Museum of the King —
though doubt has been
cast upon the pro-
venance of the nose.

The Bathers

Elsewhere it was the
Weimar Republic, where
elephants paraded & a
Zeppelin as likely as
a stork to go flying over-
head. We would go
bathing, away from the
municipal pools where
the Nazis were starting
to set up their "swimming
clubs." Found them dis-
tasteful. More to our
liking the outdoor lidos
like the Strandbad Wannsee
where we could go naked
& nobody minded. Which
is where Leni Riefenstahl
saw us, saw in us the pro-
totype of what she could
flesh out when the time
was right. Calisthenetics
as political exemplar of
the purity of the race. Of
which we unwitting, un-
aware. Later ashamed.

The Voice of Space

Not how I would have
preferred to spend
my time. But when The
World asks you to
take a turn around
the lawn after lunch
how can you turn
the invitation down.
Forwent the siesta ex-
pecting insight &
the exposition of an
ideal set of corporate
goals. Instead subjected
to an egotistical list
of mergers, takeovers,
strategic alliances, &
plays that have no
other purpose than
an exercise of
personal power. So sad
to find The World is
just another business
that is run by men.

Variante de la Tristesse

Chaotic day-
dreams. Entropic
nightmares. She left &

went uptown. The bus
was full of particulate
matter in which she

recognized fragments
of her own amino
acid chain.

Ika Loch's Bordello

Her speciality is to
assume positions in
which she holds up to
the consumer a smaller
version of herself which
holds a smaller version of
herself which holds etc. Seen
from one side it might seem
she is reducing her exposure
or possibly offering optional
extras. But Magritte quite

often shows reflections in
reverse, sees things from be-
hind as it were. Which means
instead of demeaning herself
she is actually posing this way
to gradually impose herself by
growing larger & eventually
dominate the space around. So,
no reaction from the front,
but the building at the back
is obviously excited by it all.

The Harvest of the Clouds

I am releasing My Oil of Joy
over you. Things are in
our favor this year. Sugary
sweet with a little tang.

The resource becomes scarce.
Solar panels can only take
energy capture so far. The
bezels are much smaller

than those on many phones.
Literal rivers can cross the
dimensions. Mimic what they're
trying to build. Source code

or keyboard input is displayed
as entered. The filmroll is eight
pixels taller than in the other
versions. The harvest is done.

La Connaissance Absolue

Two nights ago, on the
TV news, vision of dust
storms in the dry center
of the continent, sweeping
pinkly towards the sea.
Now they have reached
it, & brought some solid
stuff along as well. The
bird is puzzled by it all.
He's *au fait* with classical
physics; but quantum
theory is a stone too far.

René Magritte & Ursula Le Guin encounter one another

As
Ursula Le
Guin once wrote

Un objet rencontre son image, un objet
rencontre son nom. Il arrive que l'image et
le nom de cet objet se rencontrent ·

forêt

the word for
world is
forest.

L'Ange Migrateur

Mi sono sentito come
una barca sbattuta
da tante parole. I felt
like a boat slammed
by so many words,
even though this is
mare nostrum, our sea.

There was an error
when communicating
with the Annotation
Service. It was 52mm
in diameter, made of
steel, & considered
hazardous — that's

all that was known
about it. No changes
that occur at a specific
altitude have been made
to the original text. No
drive for respiration
in response to the sep-

aration of head, the
skewering of body to a
convenient table. We
cannot carry on as
before & wait for the
weather to improve. How
do birds find their way?

The Age of Marvels

The abdomen is ex-
orcised & filled with
clockwork. It is another
deconstruction, like
the distraught easel,

unlike the painting on
the easel which is care-
fully constructed & ready
to receive an occupant
in the coming week.

La Fenêtre de Mélusine

No man permitted to see
her in her bath. & yet here
she is with a menhir watching
over her. The open air is not
her natural element, but
night — & the ewer of water
nearby for safety — allows
her to partake of it. So, she

kicks her serpent tail away
& offers the promise of her
future self up to it, that
full moon riding on or in
her belly evidence of the
shapeshifting still to come.

Nocturne

Everything seems in a
state of flux. The model in
this scenario effects
a reduction in uncertainty. The
result? An equivalent period
will be deducted from
the time it takes the house to
burn. So, to escape,
the bird must venture
along the borders of chaos
& hope neither bilboquet
nor curtain falls upon it.

The perfume of the abyss

                    Incorrect to talk of the
          food chain as if it were
                    a single entity. Absence
                         blots people out. Others
               emerge, elements of a
                    sense of guilt that is
          sometimes offered up
                         as a straight radiant,
               sometimes as the center-
                    piece of a *vesica piscis,*
          the fish's bladder favored
               by some religions. The
          abyss is redolent of each
                    & every aspect — or
               would be if someone were
                         there to be aware of them.

The Poetic World

Now that interactive kiosk
projects are breaking up on
the beaches, & gay couples
no longer have concerns a-
bout big business gaining
a stranglehold over ephemera
sales, let's put on another
silly dance track & direct our
attention toward the need for
a retirement income from some-
thing outside the stock market.

The Roof of the World

I am lost, though the street signs tell me I'm at the corner of Main & Forthright. This is a part of—uptown? downtown? out of town?—I do not recognize. There is traffic on the roadway, people walking there, bodies decorated with model cars that encase their waists, obeying the traffic directions, the lights, the speed signs. There is a separate lane for pedal cars. The sidewalks are paved with astroturf.

The Explanation (2)

Father is discarded, is
dying, may even be
already dead. Freud
sits at the prestige table
offering up thanks to
Sophocles, thinking
that without the help
of *Oedipus Tyrannus*,
he may not have even
managed to get a seat
at the table nearest to
the kitchen. Mother
has another drink, says
to her son: "Now I have
the carrot & the stick in
one." Son: "*In vino veri-
tas*. Fuck you, Mother."

Magritte

ran
second in
the Rockhampton Cup.

COUNTRY RACING

ROCKHAMPTON

6 — 2000m: KOHNRAY STAR 53 (D Evans 6.00) 1, Magritte 53 (C Pay 41.00) 2, Legal Brief 53.5 (G Baker 5.50) 3. Others: Celtic Trial, Pilliga, Cearnaigh, Final Demand, Highest Power, Conspiracy, Midnight Avenue, On A High, Star Of St. Covet, Latinlover, Mycenae, Get It Good. **Scr:** 5. 2¾l, ½l. 2:02.10. **TAB divs:** Win $11.80, place $3.80, $11.80, $1.80. Q: $329.40. E: $700.80. T: $3312.10. A2: $80.20 (8-11), $8.30 (7-8), $26.70 (7-11).

Might
have won
except the jockey

left the course
& got
lost.

La traversée difficile

The eye model presented
is the stuff of legends, a
stylistically pleasing & emo-
tionally useful device in which
is embedded a sonar sensor
ultrasonic rangefinder that can
detect objects up to many kilo-
meters away. Can't always
identify what they are, though.
Thinks what we see as a storm-
battered square rigger might
be a mere rough stake, or a
piece of shapeless wood, or
even an expensive delicate ship,
escaped from some other Museum
of Fine Arts, that has somewhere
to get to & sails calmly on.

Les verres fumés

In a time of turbid
media & a weakened
economic outlook, this
display of stone tools
was put together. We
struggled with the
structure, were divided
over whether, with
the data sets that were
available, we portrayed
a goddess of resurrection
& rebirth or Fanon's dictum
that colonialism doesn't
come to an end with the
declaration of political
independence. Both
would require dark glasses
for their viewing. The one
because the brightness
blinded, the other so we
wouldn't see our shame. In
the end we compromised,
put both together, some-
what incomplete. Are pre-
paring a plaque which reads:
"Will be a lifelong pity if
having visited Tiger Hill
you did not visit Gödel."

The signs of evening

Night approaches. Upright,
uptight, the painting that
divides crepuscular &
corrugation bursts its banks.

Too much to contain, that
the same day has different
times in different places.
Maybe even a different

season as some kind of fruit
is falling. It rolls out of that
picture & into this. Gravity
strikes. Plus globalization.

No sign of source identity.
Confusing. This time of day.

The Loftiest	de Chirico's glove	memory	Arnheim	Georgette	entropy	p ↔ F(G(p))	carte blanche
sky in the eye	Game	transfix		corps de femme	Les mots et Les Images	the lovers	sine qua non
vache	Rue de la Régence	capsule hotel	mirror	therapy	sponges	giantess	
la trahison	my oil of joy	bilboquet	Truckee	dry landscape	collage		Fantômas
saber	Foucault	the empty mask	frame	Sphinx	cicerone	curtains	evening gown
oasis		9/16	mnemonic	∞	table	seducer	rêve
swarm	horses' bells	Space	je pense, donc je suis	River Sambre		Arthur Gordon Pym	narine
time	grape harvest	an empire of lights	abyss	unicorn	axolotl	diaspora	kiss

Les surprises et l'océan

There is a head shaped
like an ear that carries with-
in it a magic mirror that
may or may not hear, but
offers a diffident aspect

of the ocean. A woman in
a little black dress carries
it as she waits for dinner
to be served. The narrow
pyramids of sand are there

to snack on if she gets hung-
ry, fretting for her date to
arrive. Who may surprise her.
The sea is fairly flat, seems
perfect for galloping in on.

La Pensée parfaite

The war continues in a
linear fashion. Not so
the seasons. Here they
are condensed, all four
evident on the one tree.
A thumbing of the nose
to the man-made dam-
age that has, that will,
be done elsewhere to
the earth. We are out-
side it, says the tree. We
have the freedom you
can only dream about.

The Gun

An object	le terminus
is not so	œil de triton
attached	miasme
to its	la girafe
name	éternité
that another	le tronc d'arbre
one more	ce cavalier
suitable	campagne
cannot	philosophique
be found	la liste
to take	lambiner
its place.	le canon.

The Denizens of the River

The exteriors are thought-
fully designed, the branding
concepts unique. Much use
of plays on words. Artillery
shells gathered from the
river, clothes that floated by
in an illumination of flood-
lights, the occasional limb

artificially placed or worn
as necklace. Gloved fingers
rehearse the future journey
on a globe of trackless water.
Then the plunge, & kick to
the groyne across the river.

The Message to the Earth

This is the evidence. It is
presented in a frame so
there is distance between
the audience & the objects
they are observing. The
sponge was probably white.
Now thrown to earth / its
blood vessels broken / stain
has taken over. & petrified.
Is front of stage, before
the curtain, behind which
wires can be seen. Would
be wrong to think they
were there for telegraphy —
come from, go to, nowhere.
Part of a disquieting display
which leaves dimensions
disturbed, connections am-
biguous. The tableau is the
message, is whatever one
makes of it. But underneath
it says: *We are here already.*
You just need to learn the
language to understand that.

Memory of a Journey (1955)

In the
dark I become
accustomed
to the work
of Le Douanier
Rousseau.

It helps
that I have
a lion
beside me.

Les Jeunes Amours

Not all European artwork focuses
on Friday night shopping or offers
economic incentives for improving
the supply chain. Certainly it has
been known to promote products
from famous *parfumiers,* or use
monocled vamps who smoke a
particular brand of cigarettes. Things

not for the young, who are often
gripped by poverty. Though, as
Aristotle said, have learnt the use of
trinkets as metonomy. Throw colored
balls up into an air where they shouldn't
exist. Then bring them down as apples.

Dada Mag

ADAM DAG

DAMD AGA

MAGA DAD

AMGD ADA

MAGD AAD

ADGA AMD

DADA MAG

Excuseer, Juffrouw, is het een sprekende film?

Does that really matter? Even if the film
is silent, the continuity — or discontinuity —
of its contents, the things we are seeing,
provokes an inner mono- &/or dialogue.

Not necessarily in words. Could be images,
fragments of a past or figments of a future,
that have nothing to do with what was en-
visaged by the *auteur*, but triggered by it

even so. Could be sounds, birds on the
roof, trains passing in the night, what we
grew up listening to, what we associate
with the wider screen where they appeared.

Or maybe we approach it in the same way
we partake of a day at the races. The colors,
the numbers, known & easily discernable;
the purpose clear, but not yet the outcome.

As complement, a gallery full of the works of an
almost contemporary Belgian master which
presents a nominally silent narrative, but has
within it a host of interwoven speaking parts.

L'Espoir Rapide

Everything can probably
be remembered
but it's the linkages
& the lack of space to

keep them near that
make it difficult. Memory
is not linear. That's for
planning the future

where you write yourself
preliminary notes & leave
them in strategic places.
So that whenever it is

you arrive at wherever
you were going you can
open them up & see what
happened along the way.

The Banquet

All honour's mimic, all wealth alchemy.
John Donne: The Sun Rising

New pigments populate the palette.
All shades are considered vegan-
friendly, easy to incorporate into
your diet. Even bees are considered
sacred. Not so coffee grown in the
sun. Has been taken out from under

shadow, the natural canopy cut down
to make that so. The driver wealth,
to produce much higher yields, more
money for the grower. No hint of
alchemy, especially that part of it
concerned with prolonging life. No

natural forest so fewer insects &
migratory birds. No falling leaves
to provide compost as they rot so
more fertilizer, more water needed
to produce. Trees used to rise behind
the setting sun. No longer. No honor.

A la rencontre du plaisir

Is already awake; but is a
reflection of the Rubaiyat in
which a man in a bowler hat
stands staring into the bowl
of night. Has parted the
curtain, discovered a small

area of day on the nighttime
stage. Made smaller by the
presence of the moon.
The moon stares at the man.
Is it because of the bowler
hat? Or bewilderment at the

daytime dress of someone out
at night? The man, meanwhile,
takes note of the blue behind.
Stares at the moon. Ponders.
It's dressed for night. What
is it doing out during the day?

Debugging problems

Creating a demographic —
physical, social, & sparse
foothill pine/chaparral to
mixed conifer. There is no
intersection between bodily
trauma & foods that may
cause subcontract squan-
dering. *Magritte fragilise le*

sens; but modern accumu-
lations have also been found
in the constructed list. Please
use this display as a guide-
line only for those sites that
have since risen to the surface.

Territory

Individual human beings are very
sparse on our 12 acre property
in the foothills of Western North
Carolina. It's why Magritte has
set up here, noting that: *Même si
les objets avaient reçu des noms
différents, ils trouveraient toujours
un lieu de repos ici.* An idealized
approach, much like the view
in the rear-view mirror of my
car, where the further away
you get, the clearer things become.

The Poetic World II

Sometimes we can
make an eye-stalk

rhyme with curtains.
But when we do, any

subsequent act, like
seeking out an object

that rhymes with little
pointy pyramids, results

only in the sky cracking.
Nothing rhymes with that.

Perpetual Motion (2)

Ever since J. G. Ballard
rewrote Jarry, replacing
the death of Christ with
that of JFK in the uphill
bicycle race, nothing is
constant in the circus. Used

to be the place that every-
one got away to. Now it's
where everyone wants to
get away from. Led by the
strong man, still balanced
& leaden-faced, but has

a bone to pick with each
& everyone. Evidence all
around, reflected in a
mirror in the moorlands.
The circus has moved on.
Is elsewhere. Empty cages.

[Untitled]

La Trahison des Images — *The
Treachery of Images* — is ex-
emplified in this untitled draw-
ing of a pipe whose mouth-
piece is a penis. "This is not

a pipe" was written across the
earlier painting. There is no
writing here; nor any apparent
subtlety. Simply what might
quite easily be a sardonic dig

at an iconic painting, to bring
it down, denigate it, yet done
with all the painterly qualities
we associate with Magritte.
& it is that last fact that under-

lines the intended humor be-
hind it all, the being fully aware
of any & all implications. That,
in French, *pipe* is slang for *faire
une fellation*, perform a blowjob.

Le temps jadis

It is idle to lament inevitable progress from "the olden, golden days."

Modern techniques are a bit more complicated than those of old, when a flannel band & goose grease played principal parts in child care, & summer dwellings were modestly equipped with no electricity or running water. Childhood is growing up; & adults involved must make a conscious effort to pay more attention to it than in days gone by. It is not without its challenges. Fatboy Knäpsäck is just like his old fashioned wooden stock magical knapsack.

The velocity of the water would decline a little during the mid-winter, so scholars long ago took everything in & then digested it — the relaxing fluid texture of the herds returning from the high mountain pastures to provide the skin with a smooth & scented lather, the many agricultural & domestic tools, the Frisian water dogs once used to hunt otters.

The shed of the wine presses is full of activity. Several churches, chapels, & monasteries bear testimony to the past — the 14th century Le Temps Jadis building, the 11th century Collegiate Church of Notre-Dame, the Château de Bizy. In the old days this district was home to the Knights Templar. Here the river still follows its natural course through an old agricultural landscape where the occasional castle is a reminder of the past.

Luckily, the Sweden of yesteryear, where axes were not known & ivory & stone were used instead, is extremely well preserved. This unique & historic ambience makes you feel cast back into Mozart's time.

Le Retour de l'Explorateur

Something once seen only on
the National Geographic Channel,
now everywhere — Instagram,
Snapchat, or any other app available

from the Apple Store as well as
every cable channel on the planet.
The glorious return of the explorer,
home from the hills, the snow, the

plains, the jungle — everything's
in reach these days of sportswear
sponsorship. Though. Not always
glorious. This time, comes back, no

head, clothes torn from the back, a
speaking tube used not for voice
but for ex- or inhalation. Powder
all around. Let's say the jungle.

Les fenêtres de l'aube

Wipe your eyes with a
kerchief so the tears
outline your hand. Is
that a face reflected
there as well? Sit down
on any available cushion,

take in the view. Either
the depicted one — a
row of hills, some trees
that will return in a later
piece — or something of
your own making, still

taking shape & not ready
to be revealed, hidden
in blackness. These are
some of the sights that
the windows of the dawn
might open out on to.

Les Bon Jours de Monsieur Ingres

Somewhere, sometime, I took
this Ingres figure out of con-
text & painted around the
space that remained. That's
how I felt at the time: caught
up with inference & reference,
seeking to highlight what was-
n't there. I've moved on, have

decided to return & fill the
spaces once again, not with
the figures seen by antiquity but
as if they came from the circus
or *commedia dell'arte* — the clowns,
the dancing bears, the harlequins.

The Birth of the Idol

Here there are no judges'
chairs that turn around.
Rather, in a somewhat
hyperactive nod to Botticelli,
it is the the whitecaps that
rage & foam. A symbiotic
frenzy. They give energy
to her knowing that she'll
give it back to them when
she emerges full-grown

from this half-hell. The am-
bience is pure de Chirico
punk, whether pre- or post-
apocalyptic one is never
quite sure. Is augmented by
Magritte's props which are
stacked up ready to take
their places when later called
upon. Mirrors, & doors with
holes cut in them — a way

through a way through, a
different way of seeing. &
the idol herself, *un bilboquet
désarmé* which allows her fingers
free range to trace the template
she poises on. Is there enough
humanity within this segment
sliced from human simulacrum to
allow her to progress, given that
the stairs go neither up nor down?

L'esprit et la forme (1928)

There is much to
sing about here.

The glass of water.
The fish out of it

but still swimming
happily around. The

pawn, token of a
game she has just

learnt but is much
taken by. Which she

has natural advant-
ages in since she can

float above it & read
the play as easily as

she can read the myst-
eries of the sea floor.

Among the Groves of Light

It is an analog module in the
open air, a small thing in a
large area, high in bright light,
low in the dark. Perfectly posit-
ioned to host the most popular
fund-raising events of the year,
it reads data from many sources,
harnesses the continuous vari-
ation aspect of physical pheno-
mena to provide 16 or more

channels in the same space, uses
cookies to ensure that it gives the
user the best experience. Unfortu-
nately, in shade, branches will
wither & drop to the ground; &
the right stick has an almost 35%
deadzone, regardless of any set-
tings. Which means in this range
the in-game camera won't react
at all to its controller's input.

Le Voyageur

Botticelli lives in the ground-
floor flat. Most of the time
you hardly know he's there
except for those days when
Venus emerges, pauses, poses
on the welcome mat & a host
of classical gods & dryads &
nymphs & cherubim come
gathering around. Which, of
course, brings a crowd of mere
mortals. Half of whom continue
to gaze, & half of those think
something nefarious is going on,
& half of those think it might be
a porn video being made, & half
of them contact the police, & half
of those . . .& half . . . & ha . . . &
somewhere in the madding crowd
is a dude who's catching it all on
cell phone & dreaming of a You-
Tube video called Proving Zeno's
Paradox, & is busy looking round
for a tortoise to give that touch of
authenticity & frisson to the piece.

L'Aube à Cayenne

The tree trunk taken, & turned
into a book. Dürer is praying a
miracle may occur — as he has
done for several centuries — &
the tree become whole again. Yes,
he knows trees reach up to the
sky, but they should have a base
to support them, not be silhou-

etted against the rules of nature.
Now his hands hold a ball of
thread to tether it to the ground
if he can get his magic metal sty-
lus to draw it closer. He has to
hurry, for the candle burns away.

The Night Owl

possible , I grasp the knob within reach of my hand or almost-in order
ticed any others previously &citation1775=A fresh incident prevents me
a knob may have left some mark on it , I become aware of the real cause
time to dwell on &citation1778=I give the knob a shake &citation1779=The
does not prevent the lock from functioning normally , quite the contra
s in order not to disturb my neighbors , I sit down noiselessly in a se
tting in front of me , who , having turned around for a moment at my la
tent couple kneelng in front of it &citation1787=Aha ! This gives me e
eason !) , I settle myself more comfortably in my seat for a bit of pe
the performance by shifting from side to side on her velvet seat &cita
ng in her ear a brief résumé of the plot , which recounts-I tell her-a
at great length , then over the cliffs &citation1792=Scrutinizing the g
he bather (mentioned already) and her scanty clothing &citation1793=The
things the abnormal temperature of the little key) , right down to th
96=Now she only has to swallow the bird &citation1791=Since the bird ha
e was drinking in avidly-had been poisoned &citation1799=To the accompa
th is ill defined) not far from there , on the other side of the corrid
~'s intricate hairdo has corne undone on the way and her heavy blond ha
ion1802=Moreover the doctor in the long black coat makes an extremely t
, whom closer observation reveals to be very much less diaphanous than
=To get rid of my scanty clothing and delicate evening shoes I unthinkir
etween the tall rows of façades whose dilapidated condition has been po
of disturbingly creviced walls , bricked-up windows , gaping slits , and
midst of this demolished quarter , I notice yet again the little shop se
esses , the dummies , the trying-on cubicle , the double back and how
in the middle of the performance , I crossed the broad , dark , empty
fruiterer or drinks seller , the reddish stain marking one of the edge
lice from a tree trunk mounted on four crude legs , but one in mind of
by the spate that has brought its level up to the vaults of the arches
ng at her stomach &citation1812=I paid the small price asked for but
l he as of a large stone dropping from a great height into the river &c
tita ion1815=But I must push on , having wasted enough of the limited t
in th current &citation1816=I immediately come upon this uncertain ,
structures , derelict buildings , wooden huts , and , farther on , thi
ion buried at an unusual depth &citation1817=Nor do I stop at the chest

The Art of Conversation V (1950)

Knit & pearl alternately for four
rows. Underneath it, in white
wool, long enough to interest, yet
not long enough to tire, with the
words written in a clear, legible

hand, this note: "This is not a dream."
Written from the heart, the simple
eloquence of the words forces the
ideogram to arrange itself accor-
ding to the laws of a simultaneous

form. Avoid postscripts, punctuate
carefully. Render the outline as a
thin skin that must be pierced in
order to follow, word for word, the
outpouring of its internal text. A

lie is not locked up in a phrase, but
must exist, if at all, in the mind of
the writer. In its millennial tradition
the essence of rhetoric is in allegory.
Never point. It is excessively ill-bred.

Sources:
This Is Not a Pipe, by Michel Foucault
The Ladies' Book of Etiquette (1860), by Florence Hartley

Collage (1966) (2)

In the narrows the sun
wests. Alligators hotfeet it
for the nearest spa. The delta
stretches, rolls over onto
its back to burn its belly
& better hear the zydeco
band that bubbles by. We
spoke of foodchains, &
whether it was the
resumption of whaling
that had driven the cliff-
dwellers out of the pueblos.
He paused, pleasured by
a point he'd made, & pride
blind-sided him. The
peristaltic erudition of a
passing manatee swallowed
him up in easy pieces. Mean-
while the moon blooms
miserly in the yellows.

La Magie Noire (1946)

Antarctic winter imitated. I am
living inside a refrigerator
set up in a cold store. Beside me
there is a bird that would
escape if it could. It is my first
Assumption; & I am trying
to keep it by keeping it
as close to suspended animation
as I can. The bird is unhappy.
It is a summer bird. When
I first felt it fluttering
a few ingested pellets of dry ice
were enough to quieten it.
But as it grew
I was forced to move lodgings,
was forced to move
my chilling mode from
solid boulder blocks to
gaseous intake. Now when I exhale
my frozen breath is fuel
that drives rockets to the
moon. It does not wake the bird
but something inside it
awakens. I sense its struggles
as it recognizes flight, is
driven mad by its proximity.

Strange, dear, but

true, dear. The Cole Porter song enters
my morning mind as if it had every
right to be there, as if it lived there &
was returning home after a night out.
But not simply the song, a specific rend-
ition of it. k.d. lang's, first heard on the
Red Hot + Blue tv special & subsequent
album compilation. What is stranger is

how to interpret the locus of the singer,
of the mindsong. In the video, k.d. lang
sings as if she is person who is being
sung to; & in my mind, it is also as if I
am the recipient. To personalize, it is the
not-I singing to the other which is me. It's
a tableau that has a logic only because
of its similarity to that Magritte painting

La reproduction interdite in which a man
is looking into a mirror in which his re-
flection is thrown back, but as if seen
from the back. Twenty years ago I wrote
of this painting: "Shown from the back
the image is androgynous — think k.d.
lang in her man's suit phase." & here she
is again. Strange, dear, but true, dear.

Notes

p. 42. Photos by Man Ray, Collage by André Breton. *La Révolution Surréaliste*, no.12; 15 December, 1929.

p. 96. Magritte in 1938 next to his painting "The Barbarian" in a promotional photo for a show of his works in London. Photographer unidentified.

p.108. *writing gear*, published in Fanzine #176-2, edited by Francisco José Craveiro de Carvalho & Joana Costa, Portugal. August 29, 2021. Photo by Lauren Young.

p.122. *La Marchande de Sable*. Georgette Magritte photographed by René Magritte, 1936.

p. 303. Cover illustration by Mark Young for *The Cicerone*, xPressed, Espoo, Finland, 2005.

p. 396. Tie One On. "Last year, along with another 24 people—all male, though I wasn't conscious of that fact until I saw the finished product: gender balance, Alex, where's the gender balance?—I was invited to take part in one of Alex Gildzen's conceptual projects. The invitation consisted of a tie, an accompanying letter giving the provenance of the ties being sent out, & a request that the invitees respond with a photo of them wearing the tie they'd been sent." *gamma ways*, 2.2.2010. Photo by Lauren Young.

p. 398. Reproduction of a page from Mark Young's *Tapa Notebooks*, one of a collection of manuscript notebooks generated by nzepc activities and housed in Special Collections at the University of Auckland Library.

p. 434. *Le Principe d'Incertitude*, painting by René Magritte, 1944.

p. 461. Cover illustration by harry k stammer for *The Chorus of the Sphinxes*, Moria Books, Chicago, Illinois, U.S.A., 2016.

p. 599. From "Les mots et les images," by René Magritte, *La Révolution Surréaliste*, no.12; 15 December, 1929.

p. 604. Cover illustration by Mark Young for *The perfume of the abyss*, Moria Books, Chicago, Illinois, U.S.A., 2019.

p. 609. *The Morning Bulletin*, Rockhampton, QLD, Australia, June, 2005.

p. 616. From "Les mots et les images," by René Magritte, *La Révolution Surréaliste*, no.12; 15 December, 1929.

p. 640. Page from *La Belle Captive*, a novel. Text by Alain Robbe-Grillet, paintings by René Magritte. Translated by Ben Stoltzfus. University of California Press, Berkeley, California, U.S.A, 1996.

Acknowledgements

Some of these poems have previously appeared in the following journals:

A New Ulster, Argotist Online Poetry, Arteidolia, Australian Poetry Anthology (2018), Eunoia Review, fhole, Half Day Moon Journal, Home Planet New Online, Lothlorien Poetry Journal, Marsh Hawk Review, MiPOesias, Offcourse, Poetry WTF?!, RIC Journal, Scud, Setu, Spore, SurVision, Synchronized Chaos, Tarot, The Ekphrastic Review, The Saturday Paper, Utsanga.it, Wildlife, & *xStream.*

My thanks to the respective editors.

A number of the poems have also appeared
in the following standalone books:

The Cicerone, xPressed, Espoo Finland, 2005.
from Series Magritte, Moria Books, Chicago USA, 2006.
More from Series Magritte, Moria Books, Chicago USA, 2009.
The Chorus of the Sphinxes, Moria Books, Chicago, U.S.A., 2016.
The perfume of the abyss, Moria Books, Chicago, U.S.A., 2019.

& in the following collected / selected books:

Pelican Dreaming: Selected Poems 1959-2008, Selected & Introduced by Thomas Fink, Meritage Press, California, U.S.A., 2008.
The Codicils, Otoliths, Rockhampton, Australia, 2013.
Songs to Come for the Salamander, Selected Poems 2013-2021, Selected & Introduced by Thomas Fink, Sandy Press & Meritage Press, California, U.S.A., 2021

The majority of the poems first appeared, along with the related paintings, on my blog *mark young's Series Magritte,*
https://seriesmagritte.blogspot.com

A Postscript

I'm thinking about wanting to see *Magritte: The Mystery of the Ordinary, 1926-1938* exhibition at MOMA in NYC. Though I see it is moving to Chicago at some point. If I can't manage the one, maybe the other? I dunno. In the best of all possible worlds I'd see it with Mark Young.

Tom Beckett: *l'amour fou*, 10/15/2013